CLUES AT CAMP

"We shouldn't be doing this," Casey whispered.

She, Hector, and Gaby were inside Mr. Velasquez's office. It was deserted because the camp director, the counselors, and the rest of the campers were all in the main room for the end-of-the-day announcements.

"Was this Alex's idea?" Hector said, looking around nervously.

"Alex doesn't even know we're doing this," Gaby replied. "It was *my* idea." She walked over to Mr. Velasquez's desk and picked up a piece of blank notebook paper. "Okay, guys, I'm going to write to Ghostwriter and ask him to help us find that clue. Casey, you search around the room for any other clues. And, Hector, you can stand at the door and tell us if—"

"Someone's coming!" Hector whispered.

"That's right," Gaby went on. "And make sure you—"

"No, I mean it!" Hector whispered, more urgently this time. "Someone's coming down the hall! We're going to get caught!"

JOIN THE TEAM!

Do you watch GHOSTWRITER on PBS? Then you know
that when you read and write to solve a
mystery or unravel a puzzle, you're using the same smarts
and skills the Ghostwriter Team uses.
We hope you'll join the team and read along to help solve
the mysterious and puzzling goings-on
in all of the GHOSTWRITER books.

Daycamp Nightmare
A Bantam Book / June 1995

Ghostwriter, [Ghost] and ● are
trademarks of Children's Television Workshop.
All rights reserved. Used under authorization.
Cover design by Marietta Anastassatos
Interior illustrations by Eric Velasquez
Cover photo of snake: 1990 © Charles Philip/WESTLIGHT

Thanks to SEGA and the ⚕ SEGA FOUNDATION
and to others who helped pay for GHOSTWRITER: public
television viewers, The Pew Charitable Trusts, the
Corporation for Public Broadcasting,
the Arthur Vining Davis Foundations,
the *NIKE* Just Do It Fund, the John S. and James L. Knight
Foundation, and Children's Television Workshop.

ISBN 0-553-48247-5

Published simultaneously in the United States and Canada

PRINTED IN THE UNITED STATES OF AMERICA

OPM   0 9 8 7 6 5 4 3 2

Ghost writer

CAMP AT YOUR OWN RISK #1

Daycamp NIGHTMARE

by Nancy Butcher

Illustrated by Eric Velasquez

A CHILDREN'S TELEVISION WORKSHOP BOOK

BANTAM BOOKS

NEW YORK • TORONTO • LONDON • SYDNEY • AUCKLAND

Attention, Reader!

I will need your help in solving this mystery. As you read this book, please watch for signs like this one . This will be a signal that I need to speak to you—and you alone. During those times I will ask you what you think of certain clues or suspects. Please write down your thoughts for me in your casebook or on a piece of paper.

Thank you.
I promise we shall meet again soon!

—Ghostwriter

1

CAMP PROSPECT

"Listen up!"

Mr. Velasquez, the director of Camp Prospect Day-camp, was standing at the front of the room. He had his hands cupped around his mouth.

"Each of you needs to come up here and get a name tag," he said loudly. "Fill in your name under where it says, 'Hi my name is . . . ,' plus whether you're a camper, senior counselor, or junior counselor. After everyone has done this, we can get on with the orientation."

Thirteen-year-old Jamal Jenkins turned to his friend Lenni Frazier. "I don't think anyone's paying attention to him," he said.

Lenni, who was twelve, glanced around. The room was jammed with young campers who were all talking and laughing at once, completely drowning out the camp director's words. Four kids were standing on folding chairs and tossing paper airplanes.

"Mr. Velasquez needs a whistle or something," Lenni said to Jamal.

Just then a familiar voice called out, "Hey, Lenni, Jamal." It was Tina Nguyen, making her way toward them. "Did you guys just get here?" she asked.

"I've been here since eight," Lenni said, her brown eyes sparkling. "I was so excited I couldn't wait. I can't believe we landed these jobs, can you?"

"I heard that one hundred and thirty kids applied for junior counselor spots, and only five of us got them," Tina said.

Jamal held up five fingers and started counting. "Me, you two, Alex . . . and who else?"

"I'm not sure," Tina replied. "Speaking of Alex, have you guys seen him?"

At that moment Alex Fernandez was across the room, pouring orange juice into tiny paper cups and handing them to the campers.

"Two orange juices, please, and make it snappy!"

Alex frowned at the sound of the familiar voice. His younger sister, Gaby, was standing in front of his table and looking up at him with a mischievous smile. With her was nine-year-old Hector Carrero.

"Can I have scrambled eggs and doughnuts with mine, Alex?" Hector said.

"I'm a junior counselor, not a waiter," Alex grumbled as he handed Gaby and Hector two cups. "Remember, guys, *I'm* in charge here. You're the campers, and I get to give *you* orders, not the other way around."

"Oh, yeah, right." Gaby gulped down her orange juice, then said, "Come on, Hector, let's go get our name tags. I'm going to write my name in big, beautiful letters, sort of pink and purple and polka-dotty and . . . hey, there's Casey! And Grandma CeCe!"

Eight-year-old Casey Austin had just arrived and was lingering in the doorway with CeCe Jenkins, who was dressed in her blue mail carrier uniform. Casey was Jamal's cousin, and CeCe was their grandmother.

Casey spotted Hector and Gaby and started toward them. "I have to show them my new plastic worms," she told Grandma CeCe excitedly.

"All right, sweetheart," CeCe called out. "I'll see you and Jamal at home at about—*whoa*!" A paper airplane came flying through the air and bonked her on the head. She glared at it as it tumbled to the floor.

Hector's mother, Maritza, who was standing nearby, gave CeCe a sympathetic smile. "Things seem very crazy here."

CeCe laughed heartily. "Isn't that the truth? Still, it's nice for the kids to have this place to come to." Her expression turned serious. "We've had a lot of crime in our neighborhood lately, so I'm really glad Jamal and Casey are at this camp."

"What kind of crime?" Maritza asked, looking worried.

"Theft, vandalism, you name it," CeCe replied. "In fact, a house near us was vandalized just yesterday. A beautiful old brownstone on Portland Street, used to belong to that rich man Mr. Wainwright."

"I think I saw that on television," Maritza said. "It is a big house near the corner, with really beautiful windows, right?"

"That's the one," CeCe answered. "Stained-glass windows—they're antique, real valuable. The vandal broke a couple of them. Can you believe it? It's a rotten shame. Things are getting worse in Fort Greene, not better."

"I'm afraid you're right." Maritza glanced at her watch. "I must go now. My job at the hardware store starts in fifteen minutes."

"And I have mail to deliver," CeCe said. "Come on, I'll walk through the park with you."

As CeCe and Maritza closed the door behind them, Casey, Gaby, and Hector ran up to the head table to get some blank name tags. On the way they ran into Jamal, Tina, and Lenni.

"Hi, guys," Tina said. "So, are you psyched about camp?"

"Are you kidding?" Hector exclaimed. "My friend

Tony said this was the best camp in Brooklyn. He's really bent because his parents made him go to music camp instead."

"Music camp sounds pretty cool, too," Lenni remarked. "Still, I'm glad we're all here." She wriggled her eyebrows. "Some of the senior counselors are *so* cute."

"Yeah, yeah, yeah," Jamal said with a grin.

Just then Mr. Velasquez called out, "Could we all sit down for a minute? I just want to go over a few things before we get started with our day."

When the campers and counselors had settled down in the folding chairs, Mr. Velasquez went on. "Okay, here's the schedule. For the next four days we'll meet in this room first and last thing, for announcements."

Suddenly Jamal, who was sitting in the front row with Alex, Lenni, and Tina, felt a ticklish sensation on the back of his neck. He reached behind to scratch it—and his fingers landed on something soft and slimy.

It was a plastic worm. Jamal whirled around. "Casey," he hissed warningly.

Casey, who was sitting in the second row with Gaby and Hector, held her hand over her mouth to stifle her giggles.

Jamal gave her his best mean, no-nonsense look, then turned around in his seat.

"During the day you'll have activities," Mr. Velasquez was saying. "Two in the morning, then lunch, then three in

the afternoon. And on Friday, we'll finish up our Camp Prospect experience with a field trip to Robert Moses Beach."

"*Beach!* All right!" one of the campers called out as others clapped and whistled.

"Maybe Mr. Velasquez will let me videotape the field trip," Tina said to Gaby over her shoulder.

"That would be cool," Gaby answered. "And I could interview people for you. You know, like: How's the bodysurfing? What do you think of the hot dog stand? . . ."

"We have five senior counselors," Mr. Velasquez went on. "Each of them will be in charge of one activity. Wendy Chang will be in charge of journalism; Joe Burns, science and nature; his brother, Marcus Burns, sports; Fiona Cohan, arts and crafts; and Bones Prudhomme, music and dance."

"Bones?" Hector murmured to Casey. "What kind of name is *that*?"

"We also have five junior counselors, who will be helping the senior counselors with the activities," Mr. Velasquez continued. "Tina Nguyen will work with Wendy; Alex Fernandez with Marcus; Jamal Jenkins with Wendy and Joe; Lenni Frazier with Fiona and Bones; and Calvin Ferguson, also with Fiona and Bones."

"Calvin?" Lenni whispered to Alex. "What's *he* doing here? And why do *I* have to be paired up with him?"

"I don't know, but you don't seem too happy about it," Alex whispered back.

Lenni glanced over her shoulder and spotted Calvin in the back row. He was staring at her and smiling widely.

Lenni sighed and turned around. "He thinks we're, like, boyfriend and girlfriend or something," she explained to Alex. "I keep telling him that I'd rather get my teeth drilled than hang out with him, but he doesn't get the hint."

Mr. Velasquez glanced through some notes, then said, "Just a few more things. The head junior counselor will be Lenni Frazier."

There was applause from one person at the back of the room.

Lenni turned around and saw Calvin grinning at her and clapping hard. She sank down in her chair and tried to ignore him.

"Head senior counselor will be Joe Burns," Mr. Velasquez said, then grinned. "Okay, gang. All the campers, plus Tina and Jamal, follow Wendy. Your first activity with her will start up in just a few minutes. The rest of the counselors can spend this time getting ready for their own activities. Have fun. See you all at lunch!"

With a noisy scraping of chairs, everyone got up and headed for the door.

Casey, Gaby, and Hector fell into step with Lenni, Alex, and the others. Casey tugged at Lenni's shirt and beamed at her. "If you're head junior counselor, does that mean I'm head camper, since I'm your funniest friend?" she said. Lenni smiled at Casey.

"I don't think it works that way," Jamal said. "And Casey? No more plastic worms or any other tricks like that, okay?"

A tall, slender guy with wavy brown hair came up to Jamal. "I just wanted to introduce myself," he said with a warm smile. "I'm Joe Burns."

Jamal introduced his friends, then added, "It'll be fun working with you, Joe. I'm really into science."

"You're at the High School of Science, right?" Joe said.

"Right," Jamal replied. "How did you—"

Just then, a husky blond guy sauntered up to Joe and grabbed him roughly by the shoulders, cutting off Jamal. "Hey, big man," he said in a loud voice. "What'd you do to become head senior counselor, huh? You pay somebody?"

"Stop it," Joe mumbled, stepping back.

But instead of backing off, the blond guy moved even

closer to Joe and shoved him, hard. Joe went tumbling against the wall.

"No, *you* stop it," the blond guy growled, shaking his fist at Joe. "You stop it with this major attitude of yours, or I'm going to have to stop it for you—*understand?*"

2

A BLOODY ENTRANCE

Jamal and his friends exchanged worried glances. Was there going to be a fight?

Joe held up both hands and started backing toward the door. "Let's iron this out at home tonight, okay?" he said slowly. "I don't want to lose my job here, and I don't think you do, either." With that, Joe left the room.

Lenni stared at the blond guy, then leaned over to Tina. "Who *is* he, anyway?"

"I think it's Joe's brother," Tina whispered. She pointed to his name tag, which read:

Hi my name is Marcus
Senior Counselor

Underneath "senior counselor" were a drawing of a football and the words "I AM #1!"

Marcus watched Joe go, then turned to the group. His expression, which had been so angry before, was friendly now.

"Marcus Burns," he said with a charming smile. "Sorry about that. My big brother and I just like to kid around. Catch you all later."

"That didn't look like kidding around to me," Hector murmured as Marcus strode out the door.

"Me either," Casey added.

"I guess I'm not the *only* one here with a weird brother," Gaby remarked.

Alex, who was in the middle of saying something to Jamal, whirled around to face Gaby. "Hey, I heard that!"

"Heard what?" Gaby said, her brown eyes wide.

***

Wendy Chang pushed her glasses back on her nose and walked to the blackboard. With a piece of blue chalk, she wrote: "STOP CRIME IN OUR NEIGHBOR-HOOD."

"The *City Sun* is running a contest with this theme," Wendy explained, tapping on the blackboard with the piece of chalk. "They're asking kids to submit entries in three categories: original comic strips, interviews, and poetry."

Casey raised her hand. "Can I enter?" she said excitedly. "I *love* contests. What will I win anyway?"

"You're all going to enter, Casey," Wendy told her with a smile. "And whoever wins will get his or her entry published in the *City Sun*."

Another camper raised his hand. "Can I interview my friend Leo?" he asked.

"Only if it's related to the contest's theme," Wendy replied. "Whether you choose to do a comic strip, interview, or poem, it has to be about stopping neighborhood crime." She added, "Today we'll play around with comic strips, tomorrow we'll do interviews, and on Wednesday we'll write some poems. Then, on Thursday, you can decide for yourselves which of your projects you like best and submit that to the *City Sun*."

"Sounds cool," Gaby said.

"I'm going to go call the *City Sun* office right now and make sure I've got the contest rules right," Wendy said. "While I'm gone, Tina and Jamal will pass out sketch pads and Magic Markers, and you can all get started."

After she left, Tina and Jamal handed out the materials. The kids sprawled out in the large, sun-filled room and began drawing.

Gaby decided to do a comic strip about a character named G., a brilliant young reporter who went after violent crooks and drug dealers on her TV show, *Brooklyn Beat*. Her partner was a Vietnamese-American videomaker named T., who followed G. around with a hand-held camera hidden under her jeans jacket.

Casey decided to do a strip about a group of kids who patrolled the streets day and night to keep the neighborhood safe for everyone. Their only weapons were plastic worms, and they were called the Plastic Worm Patrol.

Hector stared at his sketch pad, which was full of scribbled words and pictures that didn't quite go together. He thought about how he had written an article last year that ended up getting printed in the newspaper. If he could do that, why was he having so much trouble now?

On an impulse he picked up a Magic Marker and wrote: "I WISH I COULD DO A COMIC STRIP ABOUT YOU, GHOSTWRITER."

Ghostwriter was the ghost of a person who had lived many years ago. He couldn't hear or talk, but he could read and write. One day Ghostwriter had started writing to Jamal, and soon after, he wrote to Lenni, then Alex, then Gaby. That was the start of the Ghostwriter Team. Only the people on the team could see Ghostwriter.

The letters on Hector's sketch pad began to swirl around and rearrange themselves. When they'd stopped moving around, they spelled: What do you mean, Hector? Why would you want to do a comic strip about me?

The camper who was sitting next to Hector leaned over

and stared at his sketch pad. "How's it going? What are you writing there anyway?"

"Oh, nothing," Hector said quickly, turning his sketch pad away from the camper. He knew the kid couldn't see Ghostwriter's words, though. Only Hector and the rest of the Ghostwriter Team—Jamal, Tina, Lenni, Alex, Gaby, and Casey—could read their invisible friend's messages.

Hector picked up his Magic Marker again and wrote: "WE'RE SUPPOSED TO MAKE UP A COMIC STRIP ABOUT STOPPING CRIME IN OUR NEIGHBOR-HOOD."

It makes me sad that there's so much crime where you live, Ghostwriter wrote.

"ME TOO," Hector replied. "I'M HAVING TROUBLE DOING THIS COMIC STRIP. I JUST WISH I COULD DO ONE ABOUT YOU, BECAUSE YOU'VE HELPED US SOLVE SO MANY CASES AND CATCH SO MANY CROOKS."

Thank you, Hector, Ghostwriter wrote. All I want is for you all to be safe!

Hector started to write something else, but just then the door burst open behind him. A camper screamed.

Hector whirled around in his seat. Mr. Velasquez was staggering into the room. His face was deathly pale, and he was holding a bloody handkerchief to his forehead!

3

THIEF!

At that moment Wendy came back into the room, carrying a piece of paper in her hand. When she saw the camp director, she let out a small cry.

"Mr. Velasquez!" she exclaimed. "What *happened?* Here, sit down." She took his arm and led him to an empty seat.

Mr. Velasquez sat down and adjusted the handkerchief on his forehead. Underneath it was a bloody cut.

"I—I was on my way out of my office," he began. "I had my hand on the doorknob when suddenly somebody burst in. The door hit my head, and I guess I passed out. When I came to, I was lying on the floor with this." He pointed at the cut on his forehead.

"Didn't the person stick around to see that you were okay?" Jamal asked in astonishment.

Mr. Velasquez frowned. "No, and there's a good reason why." He paused, and when he spoke again, his voice was angry. "The person broke into my desk and stole an envelope full of money. It was the money for this Friday's field trip to Robert Moses Beach, plus the money for next week's bike trip."

"What!" Tina cried out. Everyone at Camp Prospect was supposed to go to a sleepaway camp in the Catskill Mountains the following week. The campers and some senior counselors were going by bus on Monday. The rest of the senior counselors, all the junior counselors, and Mr. Velasquez were going by bike. Tina had been looking forward to the trip and had even started getting in shape for the long ride.

"We can still go to the beach, though, right?" Casey said hopefully. "I mean, maybe we can all bring our own lunches or something."

"No beach," Mr. Velasquez said firmly. "The money in that envelope was meant to pay for bus fares, locker fees, everything. Without it, the field trip is canceled—and the bike trip, too."

A stunned silence fell over the room. One of the campers began crying. "But I've never *been* to the beach!" she wailed. "Please, can't we just go?"

"Yeah," another camper piped up. "Maybe we can get our parents to drive or something."

Mr. Velasquez looked at them apologetically. "I'm

sorry, kids, no. There's just no way—not unless the money is somehow found by Friday."

Another camper began crying. "Camp is totally ruined!" he moaned.

Hector leaned over to Gaby. "Who would do such a rotten thing?" he whispered.

"I don't know," Gaby whispered back. "But maybe they can figure it out." She nodded toward the door. Two police officers had just walked into the room.

***

As Hector made his way to the art studio for the morning's second activity, he paused in the hallway in front of a door that read MIGUEL VELASQUEZ, CAMP DIRECTOR. The door was slightly open, and Hector could see Mr. Velasquez inside, talking to two police officers.

"The money was in this drawer marked 'Private,'" Mr. Velasquez was saying.

"Right off the bat I would guess that this wasn't an inside job," one of the officers said. "There've been a lot of break-ins in this neighborhood lately, and this is probably just another one of them." She added, "It would have been easy enough for someone to come into your office and get into your desk."

"These days a person needs more than a lock to keep anything safe," the other officer added. "You heard about the Wainwright place, right? That brownstone house over on Portland Street? A couple of real valuable old stained-glass windows got busted."

"I hate to say it, but you'll probably never see this money again, Mr. Velasquez," the first officer said.

But Hector got an idea. His footsteps quickened as he hurried down the hall to the art studio.

* * *

"A rally would be great, Hector," Gaby told him as she dipped her brush into a bucket of red paint. "If we put our heads together, maybe we could find the missing money."

Gaby, Hector, and Casey were sitting together at a long table in the art studio. Fiona Cohan, the senior counselor in charge of arts and crafts, had asked everyone to make up slogans about Camp Prospect and paint them onto T-shirts. Fiona, who was tall and slim with short red hair, was strolling around the studio, checking out everyone's T-shirts.

Lenni walked up to her friends' table and plopped down on a stool. She spread a clean white T-shirt on the table. "So what's up? Isn't it terrible about the money?"

"Hector was just saying that the team should rally and talk about it," Gaby told Lenni in a low voice.

"There's just one thing I wasn't sure about," Hector said. "Where can we rally?"

Gaby blew on her T-shirt, helping it dry. She'd painted the letters TCEPSORP PMAC, which was "Camp Prospect" backward. "That's right. Usually we meet at someone's house. But here . . ." She shrugged. "What do you think, Casey?"

"I don't know," Casey replied. "I'm too hungry to think. When is lunch, anyway?"

Gaby's eyes lit up. "Hey, that's it! We'll rally at lunch!" She looked at the wall clock. "That's only half an hour away."

"Perfect," Lenni said. She put some paint on a brush and reached for a piece of paper that was lying nearby. Carefully she painted RALLY! LUNCH.

"What does that mean, *rally lunch*?"

Lenni's head shot up. Calvin Ferguson was standing nearby, and his eyes were fixed on the words she had just painted.

"Oh, this," she said casually. "I was going to paint it on my T-shirt. It's part of this, um, rap I'm writing."

"Really?" Calvin said, looking interested. He sat down on the stool next to her. "That's brilliant. You're always full of brilliant ideas, Lenni." He leaned toward her and whispered, "You know, it must have been fate, you and I being teamed up to work for Fiona *and* Bones. I'm really looking forward to this week."

"Well, that makes one of us," Lenni said sweetly.

Just then, a faint, shimmering light appeared on the words RALLY! LUNCH. Lenni and her friends knew that

Ghostwriter was busy getting the message to the rest of the team.

"So what's up?" Jamal said, unwrapping a ham and cheese sandwich. "I take it this rally has to do with the missing money?"

The team was gathered around a picnic table just outside the Camp Prospect building. The other campers and counselors were eating at nearby tables. It was a hot day, and Prospect Park was packed with people: skateboarders, people on Rollerblades, parents strolling with baby carriages.

"That's right." Hector spoke up. He told Jamal, Alex, and Tina about the conversation he had overheard between Mr. Velasquez and the officers. "Those police made it sound hopeless," he finished. "We've *got* to do something."

"Hey, guys." Lenni put her carrot stick down, dug into her backpack, and fished out a brand-new notebook. "I think it's time to start a casebook. What do you all think?"

"Yes!" Gaby piped up.

Lenni pulled a pencil out of her pocket, cracked the notebook open, and started writing. She made sure to put down all the details of the theft.

"Hey, I have an idea," Jamal said. "Why don't we ask Ghostwriter to look for clues in Mr. Velasquez's office? Maybe the thief left something behind."

Lenni nodded, then wrote: "GHOSTWRITER, CAN YOU SEARCH FOR CLUES AROUND . . ."

She paused and frowned. "Around where?" She knew Ghostwriter could see only words and letters. So there was no way they could direct him to Mr. Velasquez's office without giving him some words to look for.

"I know," Hector said, reaching for the casebook. He wrote: "GHOSTWRITER, CAN YOU SEARCH FOR CLUES AROUND MR. VELASQUEZ'S DESK DRAWER? IT SAYS 'PRIVATE' ON IT. HIS OFFICE SAYS 'MIGUEL VELASQUEZ, CAMP DIRECTOR' ON THE DOOR."

"Good work, Hector," Alex told him. Hector grinned.

After a few moments the letters in the casebook began to dance.

"Hey, I think Ghostwriter's found a clue!" Jamal said excitedly.

Ghostwriter wrote:

HI M
SENI

"Him seni?" Lenni read. "Him seni who?" She picked up her pencil and wrote: "WHAT DOES THAT MEAN, GHOSTWRITER?"

I'm not sure, Ghostwriter wrote back.

Gaby leaned over Lenni's shoulder and squinted at the letters. "Hey, that first word's not 'him.' There's a space between the *I* and the *M*."

"You're right, Gaby," Alex said, then added under his breath, "For once."

Gaby stuck her tongue out at her brother. "Maybe Ghostwriter found part of a note saying hi to someone whose name starts with the letter *M*."

"Like Marcus," Jamal suggested. He glanced around and saw Marcus and his brother sitting together at a picnic table. They seemed to be arguing about something.

Tina started to take a bite of her apple, then stopped. Her eyes were fixed on Jamal's shirt. "Or *not* like Marcus," she said slowly. "I think I know what this clue means."

 Attention, Reader!

Can you figure out what Tina is talking about? Where have you seen the letters HI M before? How about SENI? Look back at page 11.

—Ghostwriter

4

THE FIRST SUSPECTS

Everyone stopped talking and turned to look at Tina. She was staring intently at Jamal's name tag.

"Maybe Ghostwriter saw some letters from somebody's name tag," Tina continued. "The first three letters of the 'Hi my name is . . .' part, plus the first four letters of the words 'senior counselor.'"

Jamal looked down at his name tag, then nodded. "I think you're on to something, Tina."

Lenni wrote furiously in the casebook, trying to keep up with the discussion. She didn't want Ghostwriter to miss anything.

Hector took a sip of his apple juice. "So does that mean one of the senior counselors took the money?" he asked.

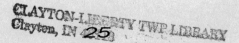

Tina shrugged. "I'm not sure. But I think we should definitely put them all on the suspect list."

Lenni picked up her pencil and started writing in the casebook:

SUSPECTS
Wendy
Fiona
Bones
Joe
Marcus

EVIDENCE
Any of them could have gone into Mr. Velasquez's office this morning. (Note: Wendy left the journalism room for a few minutes to make a call to the *City Sun*, so she could have gone to his office, too.)

Ghostwriter found the letters *HI M* and *SENI* near the crime scene, and they might be a part of a senior counselor's name tag.

Lenni stopped writing and looked at her watch. "The music and dance activity is starting in a few minutes," she said. "Maybe I could talk to Bones—you know, see if he acts like he's hiding something."

"Good idea," Jamal said. "We should all try to get to know the senior counselors as much as possible."

"I wish we could take a look at this 'HI M SENI' clue

ourselves," Alex spoke up. "That way we could be sure that it was connected to one of the senior counselor's name tags—and to the theft, too."

"Alex has a point," Jamal said. "We've got to think of a way to look around Mr. Velasquez's office and check this clue out."

"Yeah, but how?" Gaby said.

The rest of the team stared back at her. So far no one knew.

"Okay, gang, prepare to be transported into another world!"

Bones Prudhomme—a short, wiry guy with a ponytail who was dressed head to toe in black—fiddled with a dusty old record player. After a second some music came on. It was a strange and beautiful sound—full of plinks and plunks and twangs.

Lenni had never heard music like this. It sounded like raindrops falling on a tin roof, wind blowing through trees, bullfrogs singing.

"This music is from the island of Bali," Bones explained. "Does anyone know where that is?"

"Hawaii?" one of the campers said.

"That's kind of close," Bones told her with a wink. "Bali is part of Indonesia, which is part of the continent of Asia. The people of Bali are famous for their music, and they make a lot of their instruments themselves. Which leads me to my next point."

He walked over to an enormous cardboard box in the middle of the room. "In this box you'll find all kinds of *stuff*. Bottles, bottle caps, cans, pieces of wood, string, rope, old car parts, you name it. I want each of you to make an instrument, and then, later in the week, we'll form a gamelan."

"A what-a-lon?" Casey said, looking confused.

"A gamelan," Bones repeated. "Don't ask me to spell it, I'm a rotten speller. Anyway, a gamelan is a Balinese orchestra. We'll create one of our own and have a big fat jam session."

"Jam session?" Calvin muttered under his breath.

Lenni, who was sitting next to him, whispered, "Oh, come on, Calvin, it'll be a blast."

"More like a major waste of time," he replied, rolling his eyes.

Lenni shrugged and went back to taking notes on the music of Bali. She wanted to be a professional musician when she grew up, just like her dad. She couldn't wait to get home and tell him about the neat record Bones was playing.

Soon all the campers were spread out on the floor with their projects. Gaby was making a flute out of an old bamboo paintbrush; Casey was making drums out of coffee cans and rope; Hector was making cymbals out of old hubcaps.

Everyone was concentrating so hard that the room was practically silent. The only sounds came from the record player and from the occasional camper testing his or her creation.

After the music activity was over, Lenni and Calvin stayed behind to help Bones clean up. Lenni decided this was her chance to talk to Bones.

"So," she said brightly as they all got busy sweeping the floor. "Is Bones your real name, or what?"

"No way," Bones said. "*My* parents name me Bones? Ha! My real name is Beauregard. Beauregard Alastair Prudhomme III."

"Bones is definitely a cooler name," Lenni told him.

"Not in my parents' opinion," Bones said, sounding a little bitter. "The high and mighty Prudhommes." He added, "You wouldn't know it to look at me, but the truth is, I'm a rich kid."

"Really?" Calvin asked him, looking interested.

"Well, I used to be, anyway," Bones said. "My parents kind of cut me off about a year ago, when I told them I wanted to be a musician. I haven't spoken to them since." He chuckled dryly. "And I haven't had much money since either."

"Wow, that's sad," Lenni said. "It's kind of like my dad. When he told his parents he wanted to be a musician, they were real mad at him, too."

"Your dad's a musician?" Bones said.

"He plays jazz," Lenni replied. "His name's Max Frazier."

"Max Frazier, the drummer—I've heard of him," Bones said, nodding. "He's your dad? That's great!"

Lenni beamed. "I'm a musician, too. I've written a bunch of my own songs."

Calvin had stopped sweeping and was watching Lenni and Bones. He was frowning and looking jealous.

"Hey, Lenni," Calvin said suddenly. "Didn't Fiona say she wanted us to help her out this afternoon? Like right now?"

Lenni stared at Calvin. "I don't think so."

"Yeah, I'm sure of it," Calvin said firmly. "Come on, we'd better go."

"You guys go on," Bones told them. "We're almost finished here, anyway. We can talk more about music later, Lenni."

Lenni grinned. "Definitely."

✱✱✱

Tina was on her way to the journalism room when she spotted Lenni and Calvin just outside the art studio.

"Fiona's not even *here,* Calvin," Tina heard Lenni saying.

"I guess I got the time wrong," she heard Calvin reply. "My mistake. But since we're together, why don't we take a little stroll in the—"

Tina walked up to them just then. "Hi," she said, adjusting her backpack on her shoulder. "What are you guys doing?"

"Calvin was just leaving," Lenni said, looking pointedly at him. "I have to talk to Tina, Calvin—*alone*."

"Um, sure," Calvin said. "Bye."

When he was out of sight, Tina leaned toward Lenni. "I guess he still has a major crush on you, huh?"

Lenni blushed slightly. "Oh, *please*," she said. "Listen, I got a chance to talk to Bones. He's *such* a cool guy. I can't believe he's the thief."

Tina looked thoughtful. "Maybe he's a good actor," she suggested.

"I don't think so," Lenni said, a touch defensively.

"What I mean is that a 'cool' guy can still be a thief," Tina said.

"I guess you're right," Lenni admitted. "So—where are you off to?"

"I'm going to the journalism room. I think I left my notebook there this morning," Tina replied. "I'll see you later, okay?"

Lenni grinned. "Yeah, later."

Tina continued down the hall. When she got to the journalism room, she hesitated. There were voices coming from inside. She paused at the doorway and peered in. Wendy and Fiona were having a conversation.

"A group from my college is going on this incredibly

important trip in August," Wendy was saying. "It's a mission to save baby sea turtles in Mexico."

"Are you going?" Fiona asked her. Tina noticed that she spoke with a trace of an Irish accent.

"I wasn't sure I'd have the money," Wendy said. She lowered her voice and added, "But now—well, I think I may be able to go after all."

Tina stepped back into the hallway, frowning. What had Wendy meant by that? How come she suddenly had the money to go to Mexico?

Tina's frown deepened. Could *Wendy* have stolen the field trip funds from Mr. Velasquez's desk?

5

A SECRET SEARCH

"Today we're going to be making bird feeders," Joe Burns said to the campers. "Has anyone ever done that before?"

Several campers raised their hands. "I didn't get any birds, though," one boy said dejectedly.

Joe smiled and looked at the boy's name tag. "Well, this bird feeder is guaranteed to work, Lamar. It uses a supersecret special ingredient: peanut butter."

"Peanut butter?" Casey repeated excitedly. "I *love* peanut butter."

"You and the birds both, Casey," Joe told her. "Anyway, we're going to be making the bird feeders as part of a larger project: tracking the birds that pass through this park. Apparently people have been spotting a lot of new kinds lately."

"How come?" Hector asked.

"My guess is a lot of birds have had to leave their homes in the country because of logging and building," Joe explained. "They're probably passing through our area on their way to find new homes."

Joe pointed out the window, which spanned the entire length of the room. Outside was a grove of maple trees. "We'll hang our bird feeders on those branches," he said. "That way we'll be able to see any birds that stop to eat. And we'll keep track of the birds in our logbooks."

"What's a logbook?" one of the campers asked.

"A kind of notebook, Jimmy," Joe said. "Whenever you spot a bird, you'll write down the time and date and a description of the bird—like 'small, light brown feathers, long beak, white plume on head.' Then you'll try to find out what kind of bird it is by using this handy-dandy guide." He picked a small paperback off his desk. The title was *Making and Breaking Codes.*

"Oops, wrong book," Joe said with a grin. "One of my many zillions of hobbies," he explained.

He picked up another book, which had a picture of a bright red cardinal on the cover. "This is the right book," he said. *"Guide to Eastern Birds."* He put the book down and added, "If we find any unusual birds, we'll get in touch with a scientist I know who's studying this problem. So, let's get started with the bird feeders. Jamal is going to be passing out pieces of wood and some string. The wood has a hole drilled through the top of it. You're going to put the string through the hole and tie a good, sturdy knot."

Jamal started passing out the materials to the campers. When he got to Gaby, she caught his eye and pointed to a piece of paper on her desk.

He looked down at the paper. It said: "JAMAL: DON'T FORGET TO TALK TO JOE. HE'S A SUSPECT! GABY."

Jamal nodded slightly, then moved on to the next camper as Gaby crumpled up her note.

Next, Joe showed everyone how to spread peanut butter and cornmeal onto the pieces of wood. "The cornmeal will soak up the oil in the peanut butter," he explained. "That's to keep the birds' feathers from getting all gross and sticky."

The final step was to sprinkle birdseed onto the peanut butter–covered wood. "Hey, the birdseed is sticking!" Hector said. "Cool!"

While the campers were busy finishing their bird feeders, Jamal decided to talk to Joe. He went up to the senior counselor's desk and swung himself on top of it.

"What's going on, Jamal?" Joe said cheerfully.

"I was just thinking about the stolen money," Jamal said casually.

"Oh, yeah," Joe replied, shaking his head. "I can't believe someone would do that to a bunch of kids, can you?"

Jamal was struck by the tone of Joe's voice. He seemed genuinely upset about the money, and he didn't sound guilty at all.

"Well, the campers are having fun right now anyway," Jamal said. "This bird project is great."

Joe looked pleased. "I've taught lots of kids, and this is always a big favorite."

"So you're a teacher?" Jamal prompted him.

"No, I'm in college still, sophomore year," Joe replied. "I'm an environmental biology major." He added, "I've worked as a camp counselor for about as long as I can remember, though."

"Environmental biology," Jamal said slowly. "That's where you study the connection between the environment and living things, right?"

"Bingo," Joe said. "I almost majored in astronomy, but then I changed my mind. I figured I could study stars and space on my own time."

"One of your many zillions of hobbies?" Jamal said with a grin.

"Yup," Joe replied. "Astronomy, codes, puzzles—you name it."

"What about Marcus?" Jamal said. "Is he into all this stuff, too?"

At the mention of his brother's name, Joe frowned. "Um," he said after a moment, "he's mostly just into sports. He and I don't actually have a whole lot in common.

Hey, Chloe!" he called out suddenly to one of the campers. "I think you need a little more peanut butter on that piece of wood!"

Jamal wondered what was going on between Joe and Marcus. That morning Marcus had said some strange stuff to Joe about being made head senior counselor, and at lunch Jamal had seen the two of them arguing. Clearly they didn't get along. Was it just typical brotherly competition?

It was the last activity of the day, and the campers were gathered at a softball field in the middle of Prospect Park. It was still hot out, and the humid air smelled of freshly cut grass.

"All right, ladies and gentlemen," Marcus called out in his loud, booming voice. "The name of the game is slow-pitch softball. I'm going to coach one team, and my buddy Alex here will coach the other. Any questions so far?"

Gaby leaned over to Casey. "Marcus may be a little weird, but he sure is cute," she whispered.

"You!" Marcus said suddenly. He was pointing at Gaby.

Gaby started. "M-Me?" she said nervously. She was afraid Marcus had overheard her comment.

"Yes, you," Marcus said. "I want you on my team. I bet you'd make a terrific pitcher."

Gaby blushed and smiled. "Um, sure."

Marcus and Alex picked the rest of their teams. When Marcus chose Hector to be his right fielder, Hector was excited. "All right! Roberto Clemente's position!" he said to himself. Roberto Clemente was Hector's all-time favorite baseball player. Casey ended up on Alex's team, at third base.

The game that followed was an intense one. Marcus took his coaching very seriously.

"Yo, Hector, you gotta back up the first baseman a little more," Marcus told him after the second inning. To another camper, he said, "You're still choking up on the bat too much, Vida—*way* too much. Keep it down, okay?"

"Boy," Casey said to Alex when she was waiting her turn to bat, "I'm glad I'm not on his team. He's tough!"

"He's not so tough," Alex told her. "He's just being a coach. Besides, they're creaming us, so whatever he's doing must be working."

After the game Alex went up to Marcus. "Congratulations," he said, putting his hand out.

Marcus grabbed Alex's hand sideways in a power shake. "Good game, man," he said. "Sorry about scoring so many runs off you guys that last inning."

Marcus's grip was extra-strong, and Alex felt as though his circulation were getting cut off. He withdrew his hand and shook it gingerly. "No problem," he said. "So, do you

play softball in college, or what? You seem to know a lot about it."

"I play softball, baseball, football, basketball, you name it," Marcus replied, taking a bandanna out of his pocket and wiping the sweat off his brow. "I'm a phys ed major."

Alex looked interested. "A phys ed major? You mean, you can major in sports instead of math or history or stuff like that? Wow, that sounds cool!"

"Glad you think so," Marcus said with a laugh. Then he stopped laughing suddenly, and his expression darkened. "Not everybody would agree with you, though. Like my parents, right? They'd give anything if I acted more like my boring egghead brother. You know, major in brain surgery or something. They're always saying to me, 'Why can't you be more like Joe?'"

Alex didn't know what to say to that. "Well, I guess you have to do what's right for you," he said after a moment.

"Absolutely, man," Marcus said, more cheerful now. "Absolutely. And one of these days my parents are going to figure that out, too. And then they'll know who's *really* the good son." He slapped Alex on the back with a thump. "Come on, let's get these bats and balls put away and call it a day."

"We shouldn't be doing this," Casey whispered.

She, Hector, and Gaby were inside Mr. Velasquez's

office. It was deserted because the camp director, the counselors, and the rest of the campers were all in the main room for the end-of-the-day announcements.

"We *have* to do this," Gaby whispered back. "This is our only chance. How else are we going to find the 'HI M SENI' clue Ghostwriter told us about?"

"Was this Alex's idea?" Hector said, looking around nervously.

"Alex doesn't even know we're doing this," Gaby replied. "It was *my* idea. I thought of it in the fifth inning, in the middle of one of my totally amazing windups." She walked over to Mr. Velasquez's desk and picked up a piece of blank notebook paper. "Okay, guys, I'm going to write to Ghostwriter and ask him to help us find that clue. Casey, you search around the room for any other clues. And, Hector, you can stand at the door and tell us if—"

"Someone's coming!" Hector whispered.

"That's right," Gaby went on. "And make sure you—"

"No, I mean it!" Hector whispered, more urgently this time. "Someone's coming down the hall! We're going to get caught!"

6

AN IMPORTANT CLUE

Casey stared at Gaby, her brown eyes huge with panic. "What are we going to do?" she whispered.

Gaby beckoned to her. "Get over here! Behind the desk! You, too, Hector!"

The three of them crawled into the space behind Mr. Velasquez's desk. They all fit, but just barely.

"Gaby, your feet!" Hector whispered. Gaby's red high-tops were sticking out in front of the gray metal desk. She tucked them in hastily.

Casey put her finger to her lips. "Shh. I hear somebody."

They all held their breaths. There were footsteps in the hallway, and they were growing louder and louder.

"What's with this end-of-the-day announcements business anyway?" It was Marcus's voice. "What's Velasquez got to say to us? 'Hope you had fun today, bye, see you tomorrow,' stuff like that, right? Waste of time, if you ask me."

"I know, but we've got to be there." It was Alex's voice. "Besides, we're ten minutes late, and—"

Then the voices and footsteps drifted off.

Gaby let her breath out with a loud whoosh. "It was only Alex and Marcus," she said. "Big deal."

Hector got to his feet and went to the door. "They're gone," he announced. "Coast is clear."

"Hey, what's this?" Casey said suddenly. She and Gaby were still on the floor.

"What's what?" Gaby said. "Come on, move it, Casey. You're sitting on my legs."

Casey inched away from her friend and pointed to one of Mr. Velasquez's desk drawers. The drawer was marked PRIVATE, and the lock on it was mangled. "This," she said. "This must be the drawer the money was taken from, right? And look, there's something stuck to it."

Curious, Gaby leaned forward to see what Casey was talking about. There was a tiny piece of torn paper caught at the edge of the drawer.

Gaby loosened it. It was triangular, smooth on the front, and sticky on the back. On it were the letters *HI M*, and below them, the letters *SENI*. The rest of it had been ripped away.

Hector had joined the girls, and was looking over

43

Gaby's shoulder. "This is the clue Ghostwriter found!" he said excitedly. "It's a part of somebody's name tag, just like we thought!"

"Hey, you know what this means?" Gaby said, scrambling to her feet. "We've got to get to the main room right away!"

"Why?" Casey said, puzzled.

But Gaby was already halfway out the door. "I'll tell you guys on the way! Come on!"

 Attention, Reader!

Can you figure out what Gaby's up to? Why is the name tag clue so important? How can it help Gaby and the others find the thief?

—Ghostwriter

***

The announcements were over by the time Gaby, Hector, and Casey reached the main room. Most of the campers and counselors had already gone home; only a few people remained, including Mr. Velasquez. He had a fresh bandage on his forehead.

Alex, Lenni, Tina, and Jamal were sitting in the back row talking. When they saw Gaby and the others burst into the room, they stopped talking.

"Thank you for gracing us with your presence today, Gabriela," Alex called out in a deep, gravelly voice. He grinned. "Don't I sound just like Mr. Karlinsky from third grade?"

"Forget Mr. Karlinsky," Gaby said breathlessly. She sat down and showed Alex and the others the piece of paper. "We found Ghostwriter's clue!"

"Wow," Tina said after studying it. "So we were right. It *was* from someone's name tag."

"Which means that—" Hector began.

"—we've got to look at all our suspects' name tags right away," Gaby finished. "Whoever has a torn one with the letters *HI M SENI* missing is our thief!"

Jamal held up one hand. "I have a better idea. Why don't we ask Ghostwriter to look for the other half of this name tag, the part with the missing letters?"

"You mean, ask him to find the letters *Y NAME IS* . . . and *OR COUNSELOR*"? Tina asked him.

"Exactly," Jamal replied. He picked up a pen and a blank piece of paper and wrote: "GHOSTWRITER, CAN YOU LOOK FOR A NAME TAG THAT READS: 'Y NAME IS . . . SOMEBODY' AND 'OR COUNSELOR'? THAT IS, A NAME TAG THAT'S MISSING THE LETTERS *HI M* AND *SENI?*"

After a moment the letters on the piece of paper began to swirl around. When they'd stopped moving, they spelled: I'm sorry, I can't find one.

The team looked at one another in disappointment.

"Oh, well, what's our next move?" Alex said.

Gaby stood up. "Let's go back to my plan then. Let's try to catch up with the senior counselors before they leave the park!"

"Let's do it!" Lenni said eagerly. "We can split up; it'll be faster that way. And we'll rally at the picnic area after we're through."

***

"There's Joe!" Hector said to Gaby and Casey. "Come on!"

The three of them were on a tree-lined path in the middle of Prospect Park. Way ahead of them on the path was a guy with wavy brown hair. He was heading in the direction of the Flatbush Avenue exit, and he seemed to have his nose in a subway map.

"Joe!" Casey yelled out. The guy didn't turn around. "Joe!"

"He's getting away," Gaby said worriedly. "We've got to hurry!"

She broke into a run, and the others followed. Just as Joe was going through the exit gate and onto Flatbush Avenue, they caught up to him.

"Joe!" Gaby panted. "Hey, Joe!"

The guy turned around, but it wasn't Joe. He was older—maybe forty or so—and had a mustache and beard.

Gaby, Hector, and Casey came to a screeching halt.

"Oh, sorry—" Hector started to say.

But the guy frowned and took several steps toward them. *"You!"* he said in a loud, angry voice. "You lousy kids! You're the ones who spray-painted graffiti on my car last Friday, aren't you?"

"No way," Casey said quickly. "You must be getting us mixed up with—"

"I've been looking for you for days!" the guy cut in, his voice even louder and angrier now. "Just wait till I get my hands on you!" He started running toward them, his fist raised in the air.

The three friends stared at one another for a brief, terrified second, then turned on their heels and ran.

* * *

"Where are Gaby, Casey, and Hector?" Jamal asked. He, Tina, Alex, and Lenni were back at the picnic area, waiting to rally.

"Maybe they found one of the senior counselors," Tina suggested. "I wish we had. We saw Wendy just as she got on a bus."

"I found Marcus in the senior counselors' office," Alex said, drumming his fingers on the picnic table. "But I didn't see his name tag. He'd changed into running clothes; he was going to jog home."

Lenni looked up from the casebook, in which she was recording the rally for Ghostwriter's benefit. "Well, *I* saw

someone's name tag anyway," she said, tucking a lock of hair behind her ear. "It was Fiona's. And it was in one piece."

Just then, Gaby, Hector, and Casey came running up to them, panting. "This . . . guy . . . chased . . . us . . . through . . . the . . . park," Hector gasped out. "Joe . . ."

"*Joe* chased you through the park?" Alex said, looking shocked.

Casey shook her head. "This . . . guy . . . who . . . *looked* . . . like . . . Joe. We . . . lost . . . him . . . *finally*."

Jamal moved over on the bench so the three of them could sit down. After making sure they were okay, he updated them on what he, Tina, Lenni, and Alex had been discussing.

"So I guess we can cross Fiona off our suspect list," Jamal finished. "That leaves"—he glanced at the case-book—"Wendy, Bones, Joe, and Marcus."

"Well, I'm not so sure Bones should be a suspect," Lenni said quickly. She told the team about her conversation with him, including the part about his being from a rich family. "His parents cut him off just because he wants to be a musician—can you believe it? Anyway, he's a really, really nice guy. It's hard to believe he could be a thief."

"I had the same feeling about Joe," Jamal said. "Plus he was really upset about the stolen money. Still, we can't cross people off the suspect list just because they're nice." He turned to Alex. "Did you learn anything about Marcus?"

Alex shook his head. "Nah. He doesn't seem to like his brother much; that's about it."

"I learned something about Wendy," Tina said suddenly.

Everybody stopped talking and looked at her.

"It might be nothing," Tina went on. "But it sounded pretty suspicious to me." She told about the conversation she'd overheard between Wendy and Fiona about the trip to Mexico.

"Wow," Gaby said when Tina had finished. "Did Wendy tell Fiona where she'd gotten the money to go on this trip?"

"Nope," Tina replied. "And the two of them kind of rushed out of the room after that, so I didn't get a chance to ask Wendy about it."

Lenni was scribbling furiously in the casebook. "If you ask me, Wendy just went to the top of the suspect list," she said. "If only we could have seen her name tag before she went home."

Then she stopped writing. Her soft brown eyes were sparkling. "I just got a great idea," she said slowly. "I know how we can check out *everybody's* name tags."

7

TARGET: LENNI

"See, there's this project Fiona's going to have us do—" Lenni said.

"What does that have to do with the case?" Hector interrupted.

"Everything," Lenni said. "Tomorrow morning Fiona's going to ask all the campers and counselors to bring in stuff from home to recycle—milk cartons, old magazines, you name it. Then, on Wednesday, the stuff'll be thrown into a big recycling pile, and the campers will make sculptures and collages with them."

Gaby nodded. "I get it! You want to ask everyone to bring in their name tags for the recycling pile, right?"

Lenni grinned. "That's it, exactly."

Jamal looked doubtful. "I don't know. I mean, it seems like kind of a long shot."

"I know," Lenni admitted. "But don't you think it's worth trying?"

"I agree with Lenni." Alex spoke up. "It's a kind of weird idea, but who knows? And what have we got to lose?"

"You're right," Jamal said. He turned to the rest of the group. "In the meantime, while we're waiting for the name tags to come in, we all should try to get to know our suspects better. Tina, you work on Wendy; Lenni, you work on Bones; Alex, you work on Marcus; and I'll work on Joe. And, Gaby, Hector, and Casey, keep trying to track down clues. That was great how you guys found the piece of the name tag."

"No problem," Hector said.

"Piece of cake," Casey added.

Lenni was jotting all this down. Just then, her words began to shimmer and swirl around.

"Hey, guys, Ghostwriter's trying to say something," she said.

Ghostwriter wrote: What shall I work on?

"I know!" Alex spoke up. "I just thought of something. Mr. Velasquez said the stolen money was in an envelope, right? Why don't we have Ghostwriter look for words that might have been written on the envelope?"

"Like what?" Tina asked.

"Well," Alex said, and thought for a moment. "How about 'MONEY FOR FIELD TRIP AND BIKE TOUR,' or something like that?"

"Yes," Lenni said, writing down the words. She added, "And how about 'MONEY FOR ROBERT MOSES BEACH AND WEEK TWO'?" Everyone nodded.

Lenni wrote: "GHOSTWRITER, PLEASE LOOK FOR THE FOLLOWING WORDS:

MONEY FOR FIELD TRIP AND BIKE TOUR
MONEY FOR ROBERT MOSES BEACH AND
WEEK TWO"

Ghostwriter replied: **This may take me a bit of time.**

"Time," Tina said thoughtfully. "That's one thing we don't have much of, is it? The field trip is supposed to be on Friday."

"That's right," Jamal said, then glanced at his watch. "And speaking of time, we'd all better get home soon, or we're going to miss dinner."

"No way!" Casey exclaimed, jumping up from the picnic bench. "Grandma CeCe's making her special fried chicken!"

"Really?" Hector said eagerly. "Her special fried chicken? I don't suppose she's making enough for"—he paused to count—"five more people?"

* * *

During the morning announcements on Tuesday Lenni raised her hand during Fiona's speech about the recycled art project.

"Yes, Lenni?" Fiona said.

Lenni stood up. "I thought it would be a good idea if everyone brought in their name tags from yesterday to add to the recycling pile," she said.

"Name tags," Fiona repeated. She looked a little uncertain, but then she nodded. "Hmm. Well, why not? It'll add a touch of Camp Prospect to the project."

One of the campers leaned toward another camper, whispering, "It'll add a touch of Camp Prospect to the project," with Fiona's Irish accent. The two of them broke into a fit of giggles.

"That's enough, Carey and Sammy," Mr. Velasquez said firmly, then turned to the rest of the campers. "I have an announcement to make. Later this afternoon Joe will be taking you all to the Prospect Park Wildlife Center."

"Will there be lions and tigers there?" Gaby asked eagerly.

"And bears, too," Mr. Velasquez replied with a grin. "Anyway, the zoo is such a great place, I thought everyone should go, including the senior and junior counselors." He added, "By the way, Joe, make sure you make up a map of the zoo and get it copied for everyone. You can use the copy machine in my office."

"Absolutely," Joe said.

"Thanks, Joe," Mr. Velasquez said. "That's it, everyone. Have a nice morning. See you at lunch."

Alex went up to Lenni, who was sitting in the back

row writing something into the casebook. Tina, Jamal, Gaby, Hector, and Casey had rushed off to the journalism room.

"Lenni?" Alex said softly.

Lenni banged the casebook shut. Her head flew up.

"Oh, it's you, Alex," Lenni said with a sigh of relief. "I was just bringing Ghostwriter up to date," she added in a low voice.

Alex sat down next to her. "I just wanted to tell you— I think this name tag thing was a good idea."

"Yeah, I think so, too," Lenni said, nodding. She got so excited her voice grew louder. "If all our suspects bring their name tags in tomorrow, then we'll be able to see if any of them have the corner missing—"

Suddenly Alex jabbed her in the side and started coughing violently.

"What?" Lenni said, startled. "What's the matter with you?" Then she glanced up and saw Wendy, Bones, Marcus, and Joe walking by. They all seemed to be looking at Lenni and Alex oddly.

When they'd gone by, Lenni turned to Alex with alarm in her eyes. "You don't think they overheard us, do you?" she said anxiously.

"Probably not," Alex said. But he sounded worried. If one of them was the thief, Alex and Lenni could be in danger.

"Okay, gang," Wendy said. "I loved the cartoons you all did yesterday. That was super stuff. Today we're going to learn how to do interviews, in case any of you want to submit an interview for the *City Sun* contest." She added, "Each of you will have a partner, and you'll practice interviewing each other."

Casey raised her hand. "I don't get it. How do you interview someone?"

"And what are you supposed to say when someone interviews you?" Hector added.

"Well, it's pretty simple," Wendy said. "First of all, if you're the interviewer, you might want to write down a list of questions to ask the other person."

Just then Tina got an idea. Wendy was one of the team's suspects, and Tina's job was to get more information about her. And she saw a way to do it, right here and now.

She raised her hand.

"Yes, Tina?" Wendy said.

"I have a suggestion," Tina said. "Why don't we give everyone a demonstration? I work on a video news show at school, so I'm pretty used to interviews. Maybe I could interview you, and you could answer my questions."

Out of the corner of her eye, Tina saw Jamal give her a thumbs-up sign.

Wendy nodded. "Okay, sure, why not?" She sat down at her desk and waved at Tina to come up front. "Go ahead, Tina, fire away."

Tina sat down next to Wendy's desk and picked up a notebook and pen. She studied the blank page for a moment, getting her thoughts together, before asking her first question.

"So, Wendy," she said, "how did you get interested in journalism?"

Wendy folded her arms across her chest and leaned back in her chair. "Well, Tina," she said, "I've always been deeply interested in political issues. There are a lot of things wrong with the world. Writing about them, letting the public know what's going on, is one way to help make things right."

Tina took notes while Wendy talked. Then she fixed her gaze on Wendy and asked the next question. "What kinds of things do you think are wrong with the world?"

"The list is endless," Wendy said, shaking her head. "Poverty, homelessness, crime, and the environment, for starters."

Tina wrote Wendy's answer down, then scanned her notes again. "You said earlier that writing about these things was one way to help make them right," she said after a moment. "Are there other solutions?"

"Definitely," Wendy said. "I always say: Get involved!" She added, "For example, later this summer I plan to go on a trip to Mexico with a group from my college. We're going to try to save baby sea turtles there."

As Tina wrote this information down, her heart began

to pound. Wendy was giving her the perfect opportunity to ask about her trip!

"That sounds great, Wendy," Tina said, trying to keep her voice casual. "But isn't that kind of thing really expensive? How can a college student afford to go on a trip like that even if it *is* for a good cause?"

Wendy seemed surprised. She was silent for a moment before replying, "People find their ways. When there's important work to be done, money isn't an issue."

She scooted her chair back and stood up. She smiled tightly at Tina. "Okay, well, thanks, Tina. I think that's probably enough for now. Any questions, gang? No? Okay, then, I'm going to assign partners. . . ."

Just then the words in Tina's notebook began to shimmer and dance around. When they stopped, they spelled: Good interview, Tina! And good detective work, too!

Tina grinned and wrote: "THANKS, GHOST-WRITER."

Lenni was troubled as she headed down the hallway to the art studio. She was worried that Wendy, Bones, Joe, and Marcus had overheard her talking to Alex about the name tags. Of all the bad luck, having their four main suspects walk by just at that moment!

"Hey, Lenni!"

Lenni turned around. Calvin was walking toward her.

"Oh, hi, Calvin," she said not very enthusiastically.

He caught up to her and put a hand on her shoulder. "What's the matter? You look kind of bummed out."

"It's nothing," Lenni said quickly. "So—what do you suppose we're doing in arts and crafts today?"

"I think we're making paper," Calvin replied. "But what's the big deal with that, right? I mean, you can *buy* paper in my parents' store for practically nothing."

As Lenni and Calvin walked into the art studio, a loud noise greeted them. Fiona was mixing strips of newspaper and water in a blender.

"Hi, Lenni! Hi, Calvin!" Fiona yelled over the noise of the blender. "What a racket, huh? This is the pulp we'll be using for our papermaking. When you've gotten settled, you can help me make some more of it."

"Sure!" Lenni yelled back. She set her backpack down on the floor and went to check on her T-shirt, which was drying on the windowsill.

She wasn't prepared for the sight that greeted her.

Someone had poured black paint all over her T-shirt, then taken a knife and cut long, jagged slashes across the front of it!

8

MISSING!

"Look what someone did to my T-shirt!" Lenni wailed to her friends over lunch. She held it up for them to see.

Gaby gasped. "How could anyone *do* a thing like that? That's *awful*!"

"Did you ask Fiona if she knew anything about it?" Jamal asked Lenni.

Lenni nodded. "Fiona was pretty upset when I showed it to her. She didn't have any idea who did it, though."

"Who do *you* think did it, Lenni?" Hector asked.

"Yeah, Lenni," Casey said. "Did you find any clues?"

"Whoops, I almost forgot!" Lenni dug into her pocket and pulled out a piece of paper. There were splotches of black paint on it.

"This note was pinned to my T-shirt," she said. "The

thing is, it doesn't make any sense. It looks like code or something."

She unfolded it and laid it out on the picnic table. It said:

NJOE ZPV'SF PXO CVTJOFTT

"What's with this *NJOE* part?" Gaby said, pointing to the first four letters. "Do you think it has something to do with Joe Burns?"

Alex glanced around to make sure that none of the other campers or counselors was listening. Everyone was too busy talking and eating to notice them, and all the senior counselors were sitting far away.

"Maybe *NJOE* has something to do with Joe," Alex said after a moment. "But it does look like the whole thing's in code, so maybe not." He added, "Why don't you give me the casebook, Lenni? I'll write this stuff down for Ghostwriter."

"Don't forget to put down the new evidence against Wendy," Tina reminded him. She'd told the team earlier about the strange interview. "Wendy definitely acted weird when I asked her how she could afford to go on the trip to Mexico, like she had something to hide."

Alex nodded and started writing.

"I think Alex is right," Jamal spoke up. "This note definitely seems to be in code. The problem is, which code?"

Alex looked up from the casebook. "I'm trying a few codes out right now," he said. "There's the one where you read everything backward. And there's another one where each word is an anagram; the letters are scrambled." He frowned. "Hmm. Neither one seems to be working out."

"What was that code you were telling me about last week?" Hector said. "You know, the one you read about in some mystery novel?"

Alex nodded. "Oh, yeah. That was a code where you turn each letter into the letter that comes *after* it in the alphabet." He turned to a blank page in the casebook and started converting the letters, beginning with *NJOE*.

"*OKPF*," Alex said after a moment. "Not good."

"Why don't you try it the other way?" Gaby piped up. "You know, turn each letter into the letter that comes *before* it in the alphabet?"

Alex frowned. "I don't know, Gaby," he said, continuing to scribble in the casebook. "You don't know that much about codes."

"Oh, come on, Alex," Tina chided him. "It can't hurt to try it."

"Well, okay," Alex said grudgingly, then started writing the new letters down.

 Attention, Reader!

Can you figure out the coded note using Gaby's method?

—Ghostwriter

After a second Alex said, "Hey, I think this is working!"

"Told you so," Gaby murmured under her breath.

Alex continued to write, then stopped. "Oh, boy," he said, his voice suddenly serious.

"What?" Lenni said, craning her neck. "What does it say, Alex?"

Alex held the casebook up for everyone to see. The uncoded message read:

MIND YOU'RE OWN BUSINESS

"The word *you're* is spelled wrong," Tina said.

"I don't care if the whole *thing's* spelled wrong," Casey said unhappily. *"Somebody's threatening us!"*

* * *

As Lenni walked into the music and dance room, she thought about her wrecked T-shirt and the coded note. They proved that the thief was on to her and Alex—and maybe the whole team. Now it would be harder than ever to catch the thief and get the stolen money back.

"Okay, gang," Bones was saying as he put a cassette in the tape player, "today we'll be doing some dancing. We'll be accompanied by this fantastic group from Ghana, which is in the western part of Africa."

The music burst forth from the speakers. It was a combination of strong drums and loud, lively voices singing in chorus.

Bones raised his arms in the air and began doing some

steps. "I want you all to lose yourselves in the rhythm of the drums," he called out as he danced. "It's fun. Come on, everyone, try it!"

The music had such a great beat that most of the kids started dancing right away. Lenni found an open space on the floor next to Joe and joined in. Just then, out of the corner of her eye, she spotted a piece of paper on the floor.

Lenni bent down and picked it up. It appeared to be a letter from the electric company, and it was addressed to Bones:

Dear Mr. Beauregard A. Prudhomme:

This is your third notice! If you do not pay your overdue bill within seven days, we will be forced to turn off your electricity. In addition, our lawyers will be contacting you about the money you now owe.

Lenni frowned. "Third notice" meant that the electric company had already sent the bill twice to Bones. Why hadn't he paid it either of those times? she wondered.

During a break in the dancing Lenni went up to Bones and handed him the letter. "I found this on the floor," she told him.

Bones took it from her and studied it for a moment. "Must have fallen out of my pocket while I was dancing," he said. "Bills, huh?" He flashed Lenni a charming smile. "Since my parents cut me off, I've had a tough time making ends meet. But so what, right? No pain, no gain, I always say."

Lenni smiled back at him, but inside, she didn't feel much like smiling at all.

As much as she hated to admit it, Bones's money problems made him an even stronger suspect than before.

***

After music and dance the campers and all the counselors walked over to the Prospect Park Wildlife Center.

Joe, who was in charge of the trip, stopped at the entrance and held up one hand.

"Okay, people!" he called out. Nearby, shiny black seals splashed around in a turquoise pool, barking noisily. Joe had to talk loudly to be heard above them. "I want us all to go through the zoo as a group," he went on. "But just on the off chance that anyone happens to get separated, Jamal and I are going to pass out some maps."

Alex turned to Tina, who was standing next to him on the sidewalk. "I've been thinking about that note," he said in a low voice.

Tina nodded slightly without looking at him. "What about?"

"Why was it in code?" he said. "I mean, why didn't our thief just spell it out in plain English?"

Gaby and Lenni came up to them just then. "What are you guys whispering about?" Lenni said.

"We're trying to figure out why that note was in code," Tina explained.

"Hmm," Gaby mused. "Well, maybe the thief wanted to show off how smart he or she is. Or maybe the thief likes codes. Or maybe—"

She stopped abruptly. "A thief who likes codes," she said slowly. She glanced over her shoulder at Joe, who was handing out maps to the campers, then added, "Yesterday Joe told us that one of his hobbies was codes. He even had a book. It was called *Making and Breaking Codes*."

"Good work, Gaby!" Tina said. "That's a really important piece of evidence."

"I have some evidence, too, you guys," Lenni said a little reluctantly. "Against somebody else." She told her friends about Bones's overdue bill and his money problems.

"That would definitely give him a strong motive for stealing the money," Alex agreed. He reached into his backpack and pulled out the casebook. "We'd better write all this stuff down. Plus, I think that—that—*It's a really beautiful day to be outside*," he said in a loud, cheerful voice.

Gaby looked at her brother as though he'd gone crazy. Then she saw what he was up to. Joe was coming in their direction with a pile of maps.

By four o'clock the campers and counselors had made a complete tour of the zoo. They even got to see the baby elephant that had been born just a few weeks earlier.

"This was really cool," Lenni said to Alex and Jamal as they exited the elephant building. "Kind of takes my mind off the case, if you know what I mean."

Jamal nodded. "I know exactly what you mean, Lenni."

"Speaking of the case, Jamal, while you were passing out maps, we came up with some new evidence," Alex told him. "Lenni has some stuff on Bones, and Gaby was telling us that—" He stopped suddenly and glanced around. "Gaby—where's Gaby? She's not here."

Jamal and Lenni scanned the rest of their group, who were hanging out by the seal pool. "I don't see Hector either," Lenni said anxiously. "Or Casey."

"Can you guys let Joe know?" Alex said. "I'll go look in the building we just came out of. They must be in there somewhere."

"Sure, Alex," Jamal replied. But Alex had already taken off.

Lenni and Jamal wove their way through the crowd and found Joe talking to Wendy, Bones, and Calvin about macaque monkeys. Jamal told him what was going on.

Joe frowned and did a head count of the campers. "You're right—three short," he said after a moment. "I wonder where—"

But just then Alex came racing up to them. "Gaby and Hector and Casey aren't in the building," he said breathlessly. "I think they're missing!"

9

A TALE OF TWO MAPS

Gaby, Hector, and Casey couldn't tear themselves away from the enormous sleeping snake. They had fallen behind the rest of the group and then taken a wrong turn down a hallway. They ended up in a snake room.

The snake they were staring at was light brown with dark brown speckles, and its body was wrapped in a giant coil.

"What kind do you suppose it is?" Casey said in a soft voice. She didn't want to wake up the snake by talking too loudly.

Hector peered at the sign next to the snake's cage. "It's a *Constrictor constrictor,*" he said, then frowned. "Huh? It must be a mistake or something. It's the same name *twice.*"

"That's the snake's scientific name," Gaby explained.

"It's in Latin. Let's see, its common name is"—she studied the sign—"boa constrictor."

"Oh, yeah, I've heard of those," Hector said.

Gaby continued to study the sign. "It says here that boa constrictors can be as long as fourteen feet."

"Wow!" Casey said, her eyes wide.

"And they kill their prey by squeezing them to death," Gaby finished.

Casey and Hector glanced at each other and shuddered.

Just then a voice came over the speakers. "The wildlife center will be closing in five minutes. Repeat: The wildlife center will be closing in five minutes."

Gaby looked around. She suddenly realized that the three of them were alone in the large stone room. "Hey, where did everybody go?"

"I guess we lost them," Hector said. "Guess we'd better look at Joe's map and figure out how to get out."

He pulled the map out of his pocket. At the top of the page, in Joe's tiny, neat handwriting, were the words:

YOUR GUIDE TO THE PARK WILDLIFE CENTER
FROM YOUR FEARLESS LEADER, JOE BURNS

Hector studied the map for a second, then pointed to a door on the far wall. "I think we can leave through that exit over there."

Suddenly the lights in the room began going out one by one. Within seconds it was pitch-black.

"Oh, no!" Casey cried out. "What's going on? They said we had five minutes!"

"Don't worry," Gaby said, trying to keep the panic out of her voice. "Let's hold hands and get over to that exit, okay? Just aim for that red light."

The three friends joined hands, and Gaby began leading them through the darkness.

"What if we accidentally walk into a snake cage or something?" Hector whispered nervously.

"I don't think that's going to happen," Gaby replied. "All the cages are locked up—*whoops*!" She'd run smack into something hard.

At that instant a loud rattling sound filled the air. It sounded as if it were coming from just inches away.

Gaby let out a piercing scream and jumped back. "That's a rattlesnake!" she cried out. Hearing that, Casey and Hector screamed.

Gaby took a deep breath, trying to calm herself. Then she tugged on Hector's hand and started pulling him toward the exit. "Come on, guys, let's get out of this room." Hector tightened his grip on Casey's hand and pulled her behind him.

They finally reached the door. Gaby opened it; on the other side was a dimly lit, deserted hallway.

"I don't know," Casey said doubtfully. "This doesn't look like the right way."

"But this is the way out, according to Joe's map," Hector reminded her.

They started down the narrow hallway. The temperature was about ten degrees cooler there, and the air smelled of mildew. The walls and floor were made of concrete, and there were a couple of bare lightbulbs hanging from the ceiling.

"This is kinda creepy," Casey whispered. "But at least it's not totally dark, like the snake room."

When they got to the end, there was another door. On it was a red and white sign that said:

TO LOADING AREA

EMERGENCY EXIT ONLY

KEEP CLOSED AT ALL TIMES

ALARM WILL GO OFF!

"Hmm," Gaby said. She didn't look too happy. "I don't think we should go through here. If we do, some alarm's going to go off."

"You mean like a burglar alarm?" Casey said.

"I'm not sure," Gaby replied. "Something loud anyway." She pulled her map out of her pocket and studied it. After a second she frowned. "Hey, Hector, you made a mistake!"

"Huh?" Hector said.

"This isn't the right way at all!" Gaby said, pointing at her map. "It says here that after the snake room, we were supposed to double back to the bat room and go out *that* way!"

Hector pulled his map out of his pocket. "You're wrong, Gaby," he said. "It says on my map that *this* is the right way."

Gaby peered at Hector's map. "Hey, this is weird," she said slowly. "We've got two different maps!"

Casey pulled her map out. Hers was the same as Gaby's. "But why would Joe make two maps?" she murmured.

"I don't know, but I think we should follow the directions on Gaby's map," Hector suggested. "I think *my* map got us lost."

"That means we have to go back through the snake room, doesn't it?" Casey said, looking unhappy. Hector and Gaby nodded, and the three headed back the way they had come.

When they got to the snake room, they grabbed hands again, with Gaby in the lead. Gaby just missed hitting the rattlesnake cage. This time they heard two different rattles as they passed.

They were almost out when something dry and scratchy brushed across Gaby's face and pulled her hair. Gaby screamed and pulled Hector and Casey in the other direction. "What was that?" Gaby said, looking back. In the dim light she thought she could see a big pot with a tree in it. "I think that was a plant," said Gaby. "But I'm not sticking around to make sure."

When the threesome finally got outside and found the rest of the group, Alex was the first to spot them. "Gaby!" he yelled, running toward them. "Hector! Casey!"

When Alex reached them, he hugged his sister.

"We've all been worried about you guys," he said, stepping back and crossing his arms in front of his chest. "What happened?"

Gaby told him about the snake room and the two different maps.

Alex pulled his map out. His was the same as Hector's. "This is pretty suspicious," he said grimly. "We'd better record it in the casebook."

Just then Jamal, Lenni, Tina, and Joe rushed up to the group. Marcus was following them, looking curious.

"What happened?" Joe called out. "Where have you guys been?"

"What's the matter, Joe—can't keep your pack together?" Marcus said, coming up behind his brother. "Mr. Velasquez isn't going to be very happy to hear about this, is he? Ha ha, just kidding, man," he added, slapping Joe hard on the back.

"Please, Marcus, this is no joking matter," Joe said wearily, then turned to face Gaby, Hector, and Casey. "Are you guys okay?"

"We're fine," Hector said, a little coolly. "We got lost because of your—"

"—really great map, which we kind of forgot to look

at," Gaby cut in with a smile. "We're sorry if we caused any trouble."

Hector, Casey, and Alex stared at her incredulously.

"Hey, Joe!" Fiona called out from a nearby bench. "Danny here just fell and cut his elbow!"

"Be right there," Joe called over his shoulder.

"I'd help you out, man, but I've got to rush over to the volleyball nets and set up," Marcus said. "This delay has messed up everyone's schedule. My activity was supposed to start fifteen minutes ago."

"What's going on?" Jamal said as soon as Joe and Marcus had walked away. "Are you guys all right? What happened?"

Casey told him, Tina, and Lenni the entire story. Then she turned to Gaby. "I don't get it, though. Why didn't you say anything to Joe about the two maps?"

"Don't you see?" Gaby said. "Joe must have made two different maps on purpose. He *wanted* us to get lost."

"But why?" Tina spoke up.

Gaby glanced over her shoulder at Joe, who was on his knees tending to Danny's cut. "Because he was trying to keep us from working on the case," she said slowly. "You know what this means, don't you, guys? It looks like Joe is our thief!"

"Maybe," Jamal said after a moment. "But maybe not. The map thing could have been an honest mistake."

Suddenly the words on the side of a nearby hot dog cart

began to shimmer and move around. Lenni was the first to notice it.

"Ghostwriter's trying to tell us something," she said to her friends in a low voice.

When the words stopped rearranging themselves, they spelled:

ROBER M BEA AND BIK
PROPERTY OF CAMP PROSPECT
DON'T BE A LITTERBUG!

Hector frowned. "What a weird message!"

"'ROBER M BEA AND BIK,'" Gaby said slowly. "That looks so familiar."

 Attention, Reader!

Can you figure out what 'ROBER M BEA AND BIK' means? It looks as if some letters need to be filled in.

—Ghostwriter

10

"ROBER M BEA AND BIK"

Jamal, Lenni, and Tina were sitting in the junior counselors' office staring at the casebook, trying to figure out
Ghostwriter's message. Alex, Gaby, Hector, and Casey had
gone off to their sports activity.

Suddenly Tina's face lit up. "I think I've got it!"

Jamal and Lenni looked at her eagerly. "Well?" Jamal
said.

Tina flipped through the casebook. "Here," she said
triumphantly. "Yesterday we asked Ghostwriter to look for
some words that might have been on the envelope containing the money." She added, "I bet 'ROBER M BEA AND
BIK' is really 'ROBERT MOSES BEACH AND BIKE
TOUR.'"

Lenni grinned. "That's it! Tina, you're brilliant!"

"Definitely," Jamal agreed. Then he frowned. "But why didn't Ghostwriter just write the whole thing out instead of 'ROBER M BEA AND BIK'? And what does that other stuff mean?"

Tina flipped through the casebook again. "'Property of Camp Prospect' and 'Don't be a litterbug,'" she read out loud. "What do those words have to do with Robert Moses Beach and the bike tour?"

"You know what the word *litterbug* reminds me of?" Lenni said. "Trash."

"Trash," Jamal repeated. "That makes sense. I mean, that's what a litterbug is—someone who doesn't bother using a trash can."

"I bet Ghostwriter saw the letters 'ROBER M BEA AND BIK' in a trash can!" Lenni said. "Except, which trash can? There must be a million of them in Brooklyn."

"Maybe that's where the 'Property of Camp Prospect' part comes in," Jamal suggested. "Ghostwriter could have found the clue in a trash can right here in this building. Or even right here in this—"

Jamal stopped talking and whirled around in his chair. Lenni and Tina did the same.

Lenni spotted the trash can first. It was large and gray and painted with the words: PROPERTY OF CAMP PROSPECT. DON'T BE A LITTERBUG!

"Yes!" she cried out. She jumped out of her chair and

ran over to it. "Oh," she said after a moment, sounding disappointed. "There's nothing in here but a really old-looking jelly doughnut—yuck!"

"Let's try the other trash cans in this building," Tina suggested. "There must be one in every room."

"Sure," Lenni said, still staring in disgust at the doughnut. "I just hope we don't have to dig through too much garbage to find what we're looking for!"

***

When they got to the senior counselors' office, the door was closed. Jamal raised his hand and knocked on it softly.

When there was no reply, he put his ear to the door. "I don't think anyone's in there," he whispered to his friends.

He put his hand on the doorknob and turned it. The office was empty.

"Tina, why don't you and I go in and look around?" Jamal suggested. "Lenni, you keep guard at the door. If anyone comes down the hall, keep them out of here, okay? Make up some story."

"Sure," Lenni said. "That's me—Lenni Frazier, master storyteller."

Jamal and Tina went inside. They spotted a trash can in the corner of the room. The words PROPERTY OF CAMP PROSPECT. DON'T BE A LITTERBUG! were shimmering brightly.

"Ghostwriter!" Tina whispered.

She and Jamal ran to the trash can. Ghostwriter was

lighting up a piece of paper that was underneath some other papers.

Tina reached inside and pulled the piece of paper out. On it were some letters and numbers written in black Magic Marker. But someone had spilled grape juice on it, and a lot of the letters and numbers had washed away. All that was left was this:

ROBER   M   BEA   AND BIK
$$$
Bus f re $4 0.00
 unch $200.0
Sna ks $1   .00
 ockers $ 40.00
                _____
                $740.00

Bik rental (2) $10 .00
Cam ing fee $ 50.0
Fo d $30 .00
Sn cks $ 50.00
                _____
                $500.00

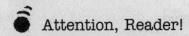 Attention, Reader!

You already know that "ROBER M BEA" is "ROBERT MOSES BEACH" and "BIK" is "BIKE TOUR." How about the other words and numbers? Can you fill them in, too?

—Ghostwriter

"How are we supposed to be able to read this thing?" Jamal grumbled. "It's been attacked by grape juice!"

"I bet we can still read it, though," Tina said confidently. She studied the piece of paper. "Let's see, the three dollar signs must mean that these are the costs for the Robert Moses Beach field trip and the bike tour."

"Definitely," Jamal said. "The top half must be the costs for the field trip, and the bottom half must be the costs for the bike tour."

After a few minutes Tina and Jamal had the entire thing figured out:

ROBERT MOSES BEACH AND BIKE TOUR
$$$

Bus fare	$400.00
Lunch	$200.00
Snacks	$100.00
Lockers	$ 40.00
	$740.00

Bike rental (2)	$100.00
Camping fee	$ 50.00
Food	$300.00
Snacks	$ 50.00
	$500.00

Jamal slapped his knee. "Yes!" he said excitedly. "We've got to show this to Mr. Velasquez right away, Tina. It's *got* to be connected to the missing money."

"You know what this means?" Tina said. "Since we found this paper in the senior counselors' office, it's the first real proof we have that ties the theft to the senior counselors."

"Yeah," Jamal said. "The problem is, which senior counselor? Is it Joe?"

"I wish we knew," Tina said, and sighed.

✳ ✳ ✳

The team was gathered around its usual picnic table. Camp was over for the day, and the area was deserted except for a few pigeons eating crumbs off the grass.

Jamal was telling everyone about finding the new clue. "Tina, Lenni, and I took it to Mr. Velasquez right away," he said. "He got really excited. He said the last time he saw it, it was clipped to the envelope containing the field trip and bike tour money."

"So whoever stole the money *unclipped* the piece of paper and threw it in the trash," Tina explained.

"Mr. Velasquez called all the senior counselors in," Lenni went on. "He announced that Jamal and Tina and I had found the thing and asked if any of them recognized it. They all said no."

"Did any of them act real guilty or anything?" Hector piped up.

85

Tina looked thoughtful. "Not really," she said after a moment. "They all seemed kind of uncomfortable, though. Mr. Velasquez was pretty mad."

"We should be writing all this stuff down for Ghostwriter." Gaby spoke up. "Who's got the casebook?"

"Me," Jamal said. He reached into his backpack. "It's right in—hey, what's this?"

He pulled a crumpled piece of paper out of his bag. He smoothed it out and laid it on the table.

Alex whistled. "Looks like another note from you know who," he remarked.

It said:

SGHR HR XNT'QD KZRS VZQMHMF

"How did it get into your backpack?" Casey asked Jamal.

"I have no idea," he said. "Someone must have slipped it in there when I wasn't looking." Jamal added, "This is a good sign, though. It means the thief is definitely one of the senior counselors. Whoever it was got nervous when we turned in the new clue to Mr. Velasquez."

Alex reached over and got the casebook out of Jamal's backpack. He pulled a pen out of his pocket and started trying to decode the note.

"Maybe the thief used the same code as before," he said as he wrote. "You know, the one where you turn each letter into the letter that comes before it in the alphabet." Then

86

he frowned. "Hmm. *RFGQ.* Not good."

"How about trying it the other way?" Gaby suggested. "You know, turn each letter into the letter that comes *after* it in the alphabet?"

Alex looked up from the casebook and studied his sister. "Yeah, why not?" he said after a moment. "You were right about the code thing yesterday."

 Attention, Reader!

Can you figure out the coded note using Gaby's method?

—Ghostwriter

Alex scribbled in the casebook for a moment. Then he held it up for everyone to see. The message read:

THIS IS YOU'RE LAST WARNING

"Our last warning before what?" Casey murmured anxiously.

"Hey, guys, check this out!" Tina exclaimed. She was peering intently at the casebook. "Compare this note with the one we got yesterday."

NJOE ZPV'SF PXO CVTJOFTT
MIND YOU'RE OWN BUSINESS

"I don't get it," Hector said, looking puzzled. "What are you talking about, Tina?"

"The spelling mistakes," Tina said. "The thief spelled *your* wrong both times. It's supposed to be *y-o-u-r*, not *y-o-u-apostrophe-r-e.*"

"Oh, yeah," Lenni said. Then she frowned. "Oh, *no.*"

"What, Lenni?" Jamal asked her.

"That's another clue that points to him," Lenni mumbled.

"Points to *who*?" Hector said.

"Yesterday during music and dance he told us that he was a terrible speller," Lenni went on, talking more to herself than to the others.

"*Who*, Lenni?" Gaby prodded her.

Lenni sighed. "Bones."

DESTRUCTION

Wednesday morning was cool—more like autumn than summer. As Lenni walked down Portland Street on her way to Camp Prospect, she kept wishing she'd worn something heavier than her baggy shorts and a T-shirt. She did a few dance steps and jumps, trying to stay warm.

Then she stopped and gazed up at the sky. It was getting dark and cloudy, threatening rain.

If it rains today, then maybe the sky will be all rained out and it'll be nice on Friday, for the beach, Lenni thought. *That is, if we find the thief and the money so we can go to the beach.*

Lenni crossed her fingers as she mulled this over. With luck, one of the team's suspects would turn in a name tag with the letters *HI M SENI* missing. Then the thief would be caught, and the money would be recovered. And then they all could go to the beach on Friday and the bike tour next week.

Lenni continued walking. Halfway down the block she paused in front of an elegant brownstone house. It looked as if it had been broken into recently. A window was smashed, and across the front entrance was some yellow tape with the words POLICE SCENE—DO NOT CROSS.

Something about the words POLICE SCENE made Lenni shudder. She wondered what had happened here—a robbery? A murder? Then she remembered reading something in the newspaper about a historic old brownstone that had been vandalized a few days ago, upsetting all the neighbors. Could this be the house?

Lenni shrugged, then went on her way. The place was a little spooky-looking, and besides, she was in a hurry to get to Camp Prospect. Today was the day people would be bringing in stuff to recycle for arts and crafts—including their name tags.

Something on the sidewalk in front of the house caught her eye. She bent down to pick it up. It was a small, heart-shaped piece of colorless glass. It was outlined in dull silver-colored metal, and it was slightly chipped.

This would be perfect for the recycling pile, Lenni thought. *It would be cool as part of a sculpture or maybe a—*

But Lenni's thoughts were interrupted by sudden footsteps coming up behind her.

Before she had a chance to turn around, a man's voice called out: "Hey! What did you just pick up?"

Something about the voice made a shiver go up Lenni's spine. Without glancing back, she started walking very fast.

"Hey!" the voice called out angrily. "Hey, wait a minute!"

Lenni broke into a run.

***

"So did the guy follow you all the way to camp?" Gaby asked Lenni anxiously.

Gaby, Lenni, Hector, and Casey were in the art studio, sifting through the recycling pile for name tags. Dozens of them were mixed in with empty cereal boxes, coffee cans, pieces of junk mail, and other items. The only other people in the room were a few of the campers and Fiona and Calvin, who were busy passing out art supplies.

"I don't think he followed me very far at all," Lenni replied. "I turned around when I got to the park, and there was no one there."

"What do you think he wanted?" Hector asked her.

"I don't know. I think he was just some creep trying to scare me." Lenni shuddered and added, "Let's change the subject, okay? Anyone find anything yet?" The others shook their heads.

Gaby picked up a grungy old pair of high-tops. "Yuck!"

"Hey, watch what you say," Hector told her. "Those used to be my favorite shoes." He added, "At least *I* brought something. Did any of you?"

"Sure," Lenni replied. "I found this neat thing on Portland Street this morning, right before that awful man started bugging me. A cool little piece of heart-shaped glass. It's in here somewhere, unless one of the campers already got it—"

"Excuse me, Lenni."

Lenni turned around. Fiona was standing right behind her, smiling at her. She looked a little tense. "We're going to be starting in just a few minutes," she said. "Maybe you could help Calvin and me pass out supplies."

"Oh, sure," Lenni said. When Fiona had walked away, Lenni whispered to her friends: "Come on, we've got to speed this up. The only name tag we've found is Marcus's, and his doesn't have any letters missing."

"Right," Hector whispered back. "We still have to find Joe's, Wendy's, and Bones's."

"Here's Joe's!" Casey pointed to a name tag that was lying under an empty egg carton. "Oh," she said, frowning. "It doesn't have any missing letters, either."

"That's so weird," Gaby said. "I was so *sure* he was the thief."

"We won't find Wendy's or Bones's name tag," Lenni said. "She told me this morning that she lost hers. And Bones said his got put through the wash."

"So does this mean Joe and Marcus are off the suspect list?" Hector said.

"I guess so," Lenni replied. "And I guess it means Wendy and Bones are our major suspects now." But she sounded uncertain.

"Maybe we'd better rally at lunch and talk about this," Gaby suggested, glancing over her shoulder. "Fiona's giving you a look, Lenni. You'd better get to work."

"Whoops, okay," Lenni said, and headed for the supply closet.

***

"Okay, let's go over our suspects one more time," Jamal said, taking a bite out of his cheese sandwich.

Lenni got the casebook out and turned to the suspects and evidence page. "Wendy," she read out loud. "She suddenly got money for the trip to Mexico, and she acted weird when Tina asked her about it yesterday. Plus she didn't turn in a name tag."

"Then there's Bones," Hector said. "He told Lenni he was broke. He's a bad speller, and the word *your* was spelled wrong in the two notes we got. And he didn't turn in a name tag."

Alex drummed his fingers on top of the picnic table. "Our third suspect is Joe. He's a code freak, and the two notes were in code. Then there was the thing with the map mix-up at the wildlife center."

"But we know that that could have been an honest mistake," Tina reminded everyone. "Joe might have made one map that was correct and one that wasn't, then accidentally photocopied both."

"Right," Jamal said. "Plus Joe's name tag checks out. No missing letters. And Marcus, our last suspect, had no missing letters either." He glanced around. "Speaking of missing, where's Casey?"

Just then Casey came running around the corner of the Camp Prospect building. "Sorry I'm late," she said breathlessly, setting her brown paper lunch bag on the picnic table. "Guess what?"

"What?" Lenni said.

"I'm a genius," Casey declared, her brown eyes twinkling. "I found out something really important!"

Jamal grinned at her. "Oh, Ms. Genius? And what would that be?"

"I just overheard Wendy talking on the pay phone to her dad," Casey said. "She was telling him that he *had* to pay for her trip to Mexico because if she didn't go, she couldn't graduate. I guess he said yes because when she hung up she said something to herself like 'Great, he fell for it!'"

"So *that's* how Wendy was going to get money for the trip," Tina said slowly. "No wonder she acted so weird when I asked her about it."

"Yeah, lying to your parents isn't exactly something to be proud of," Alex remarked.

"Good work, Casey," Jamal told her. "Now we've got one less suspect to worry about."

* * *

"Now explain to me what this opening thing is again," Alex said to Lenni.

It was the end of the lunch hour, and the two of them were walking down the hall toward the art studio. Jamal, Tina, Hector, Casey, and Gaby were close behind.

"The campers spent the morning turning all that recycling stuff into works of art," Lenni explained patiently. "Fiona wanted to have an opening to show everyone's projects to the public."

"And we're the public?" Alex said, looking amused. "Me, Jamal, Tina, Bones, Wendy, Marcus, Joe, and Mr. Velasquez?"

Lenni glared at him. "You'd better say something nice about everyone's projects, or you're not going to get any juice and cookies." She added, "That's what Fiona's serving. She told us they have food and stuff at real art openings."

Gaby caught up to them. "Wait till you see my sculpture, Alex," she said. "I made a big Mad Hatter out of old magazine articles and papier-mâché paste."

"Alex, Gaby." Lenni had come to a sudden halt in front of the art studio door. "Something's really wrong."

Alex and Gaby joined Lenni and glanced in the doorway. Fiona was sitting at her desk in tears, and Mr. Velasquez was trying to calm her down. The other senior counselors were also there, as were Calvin and about half the campers.

Then Alex, Gaby, and Lenni saw what Fiona was so upset about. All around the room, the works of art the campers had made lay smashed and torn on the floor. Someone had destroyed every single one of them!

12

IN HOT PURSUIT

"Who on earth would do such a thing?" Mr. Velasquez asked angrily.

Fiona was crying. "Everyone worked so hard on their projects," she said.

"When did this happen?" Tina asked Bones. She, Jamal, Hector, and Casey had walked into the room and immediately taken in the scene.

Bones shrugged. "I don't know. Fiona found it like this just a few minutes ago. What a bummer, huh?"

"I say some kid with a major rage problem took a bat to the place," Marcus spoke up. "I mean, look at this, man! It's like a tornado came through!"

Gaby knelt in front of what was left of her sculpture. "My poor Mad Hatter," she said, sifting through the rubble. "I wonder if I can put you back together again, like Humpty Dumpty?"

"Do you think the thief did this?" Casey whispered to Jamal.

"It looks like it," he whispered back. "Probably trying to scare us away from the case."

"I'm calling an emergency meeting," Mr. Velasquez said gravely. "I'd like two or three of the junior counselors to stay and clean up this mess. I want the rest of you in the main room right away."

"I think I'd better go to this meeting," Calvin said to no one in particular. "It sounds pretty important."

"He just wants to get out of cleaning up," Lenni murmured to Tina. She raised her hand. "I'll stay, Mr. Velasquez. And Tina and Alex want to stay, too."

When everyone had left the room, Alex turned to Lenni. "Gee, thanks for volunteering me. I really appreciate that."

"Oh, come on, Alex," Lenni chided him. "Which would you rather do, go to a boring old meeting or look around this room for clues?"

"Smart thinking, Lenni," Tina said. "Come on, guys, let's split up and comb through this mess."

"The word *mess* doesn't even begin to cover it," Alex grumbled, stepping carefully over a huge pile of shredded cardboard. "It's more like a disaster area."

After a few minutes of searching, Tina said, "This is

going to take forever, isn't it? There's too much stuff here."

"Yeah," Alex said slowly. "But maybe not. Come here and check this out."

Tina and Lenni went to his side. Alex was peeling off a piece of paper that had been taped to the side of a sculpture that Lenni had made.

"I think it's another note from our favorite pen pal," he announced.

He unfolded the piece of paper. It said:

THIS IS YOUR FINAL CHANCE.
GIVE IT UP.

"Give *what* up?" Lenni said, looking confused. "What is this person *talking* about?"

Alex pulled the casebook out of his backpack and opened to the page with the other two notes.

NJOE ZPV'SF PXO CVTJOFTT
MIND YOU'RE OWN BUSINESS

SGHR HR XNT'QD KZRS VZQMHMF
THIS IS YOU'RE LAST WARNING

Alex then copied the new message just below them. "Wait a second," he murmured. "There's something weird going on here."

 Attention, Reader!

Can you figure out what Alex is talking

about? How is this new note different
from the other two notes?

—Ghostwriter

"You're right, Alex," Tina said. "The thief spelled the word 'your' *right* this time. Plus, the note isn't in code." She frowned. "I wonder why?"

"Maybe the thief got tired of having to think up new codes," Lenni suggested.

"That's possible," Tina murmured. "But I wonder if— if—"

"If what?" Alex prompted her. Tina had stopped talking and was gazing at something on the floor.

"Tina?"

"Look!" Tina said, pointing to a crumpled collage. In one corner of it, a camper had pasted in a name tag that read:

HI MY NAME IS . . . MARCUS
SENIOR COUNSELOR

Lenni shrugged. "You mean, Marcus's name tag? I've seen it already. There aren't any letters missing from it, so he's in the clear."

Tina shook her head. "No, he's not."

Attention, Reader!
Please take a look at Marcus's name tag

on page 11. What do you notice about it?
—Ghostwriter

"I saw Marcus's name tag on Monday, during orientation," Tina went on. "I noticed it because under his name and the words 'SENIOR COUNSELOR,' he had a picture of a football and then 'I AM THE GREATEST' or 'I AM #1,' something like that."

"I don't get it," Alex said, frowning. "He redid his name tag?"

"Yes!" Lenni said suddenly. "Don't you see, Alex? He must have overheard us talking about the missing piece of the name tag and how it was a clue to the thief. So he redid his name tag and brought it in, so we wouldn't suspect him anymore. The problem was, he didn't make his new name tag exactly the same as his old name tag."

Alex stared at Lenni, then at Tina. "We've got to tell the others right away," he said.

***

"We don't have *time* for a rally," Gaby said impatiently. "Hector and Casey and Lenni and I have to get to music and dance like *right this second*!"

The Ghostwriter Team was gathered in the junior counselors' office. The emergency meeting called by Mr. Velasquez had just wrapped up, and all the campers were on their way to the music and dance room. Alex, Lenni, and Tina had intercepted Jamal, Gaby, Hector, and Casey in the hallway.

"Don't you understand what Tina just told you, Gaby?" Alex said. "The fact that Marcus handed in a different name tag could mean he's the thief!"

"Oh," Gaby said. Then her eyes widened. *"Oh!"*

"The question is, what do we do now?" Jamal said. "We still don't have any real proof against him. And I don't want to go to Mr. Velasquez unless—"

Tina held her finger to her lips just then. "Shh. I hear footsteps in the hallway," she whispered.

She tiptoed softly to the doorway and peeked outside. "It's Marcus," she called over her shoulder. "He just went into the senior counselors' office. He had some sort of an envelope in his hand."

Just then the letters on a wall poster began to glow wildly. "Look!" Hector said, pointing. "Ghostwriter!"

WHAT MAKES A GOOD CAMP COUNSELOR? HERE ARE TEN THINGS . . . became

Hurry! Washington Lincoln Hamilton Jackson Grant Franklin

"Why is Ghostwriter telling us the names of U.S. presidents?" Lenni said, looking confused.

"Benjamin Franklin wasn't a president," Gaby cor-

rected her. "And neither was Alexander Hamilton. He was the first U.S. secretary of the treasury."

Jamal studied Ghostwriter's message intently. "I think I know what he's trying to tell us," he said after a moment. "Washington's on the one-dollar bill, Lincoln's on the five, Hamilton's on the ten, and so on. All these guys are on United States money!"

"Money," Alex repeated. "As in—"

"—the stolen money," Gaby said. "I think Ghostwriter just found it for us. Come on, guys, let's go!"

The seven of them rushed over to the senior counselors' office. The door was closed.

Jamal flung it open. "Okay, Marcus," he said loudly.

Marcus was just slipping an envelope into one of the desks. He glanced up, looking startled. "Oh, hi, guys," he said nervously. "I, uh—that is, I'm sorry you had to see this."

"See what?" Lenni spoke up.

Marcus held up the envelope. "This," he said, sounding a little more confident now. "I hate to say it, but I think my brother's a thief. I found this envelope of money in his desk."

"I don't think so, Marcus," Alex told him. "Tina saw you carrying that envelope into this room."

Marcus's mouth dropped open. Then he narrowed his eyes. "So that's how you're playing this, huh?" he said in a low, mean voice. "You stupid little detectives—I warned you to stay out of this!"

With that he made a sudden move. With the envelope clutched tightly in his right hand, he ran for the door.

In that split second Alex leaped into Marcus's path and tried to stop him. He imagined an announcer's voice saying, "Alejandro Fernandez, the rookie cornerback, tackles the powerful veteran receiver Marcus Burns and saves the game!"

But Alex didn't get very far. Marcus stiff-armed him, and Alex went tumbling to the floor.

"Alex!" Gaby cried out. "Alex, are you okay?"

"I'm fine," Alex grumbled, getting to his feet. "I just slipped, that's all."

Marcus had disappeared through the door. "He's getting away, you guys!" Lenni said urgently.

The seven of them rushed into the hallway. Marcus was at the end of the hall and sprinting around the corner.

"Casey and Hector, you get Mr. Velasquez and let him know what's going on," Jamal said quickly. "Lenni, Tina, Alex, and Gaby, come on!"

The five of them took off. Once they were around the corner, they saw Marcus going through a door marked STAIRS.

"He's heading for the basement!" Tina said breathlessly as she ran. "Why would he do that?"

"There's a way to get out of the building through the

laundry room," Jamal replied, trying to speed up. "I saw some kids using that exit the other day."

They reached the dimly lit stairwell and raced down the steps. They soon found themselves in a lime green hallway.

"There!" Jamal shouted, pointing to a doorway off to the right.

When Jamal and his friends burst into the laundry room, they were greeted by the sounds of washing machines and the soapy smell of detergent. Marcus was halfway across the room and heading for a wide door marked EXIT TO STREET.

Lenni started after Marcus, then came to a sudden halt. She flung her arms out at her sides to hold her friends back.

"Lenni, Lenni, *Lenni*!" Alex said in exasperation. "He's getting away!"

"No, he's not," Lenni announced. "See?"

She pointed to a small yellow sign on the linoleum floor in front of Marcus. It said CAUTION—WET FLOOR.

But Marcus was in too much of a hurry to notice the sign. He ran right past it—and his feet slid out from under him.

"Whooooah!" he shouted as he tumbled to the floor. "Help!" The envelope he'd been holding flew out of his hand and landed just inches away from the team.

Alex stooped over and picked it up. "Thanks, *man*," he called out to Marcus.

Mr. Velasquez came running into the room, followed by Casey and Hector—and the janitor.

"Who's messing up my clean floor?" the janitor barked out before anyone could say anything. He waved a wrinkled hand at Marcus, who was floundering around helplessly on the slippery surface. "You, there, young man, I want you to get a mop and do it over!"

"I'm afraid Marcus won't have much time for mopping, Fred," Mr. Velasquez told the janitor grimly. "He's got a little appointment with the police."

EPILOGUE

"Help!"

Gaby and Tina were screaming and jumping up and down as a wave came crashing toward them. They dived into the water, then emerged seconds later, sputtering and laughing.

Alex watched them for a moment, then lay back down on his towel and closed his eyes. "Can you believe those two?" he murmured to Jamal, who was on the towel next to him. "Now *this* is the way you're supposed to enjoy the beach."

"I'm just glad we can enjoy the beach at all," Jamal said, squinting up at the bright blue sky. "I mean, what if we hadn't caught Marcus?"

"I know."

Alex and Jamal propped themselves up on their

elbows. Mr. Velasquez was walking toward them, looking very pale in his baggy Hawaiian print swimming trunks.

"I just wanted to thank you all for a job well done," Mr. Velasquez said, pushing his reflector sunglasses up his nose. "If it weren't for you kids, we would have had to cancel this field trip—and the bike tour next week, too."

"No problem," Alex said, smiling. "It was a piece of cake, really."

Lenni came up to them, followed by Hector and Casey. "The hot dog stand is a mob scene," she complained. "But the wait was worth it—oh, hi, Mr. Velasquez." She held up a chili dog, grinned, and took a bite.

"Did Marcus confess to everything?" Jamal asked Mr. Velasquez.

The camp director nodded. "I saw Marcus and his parents yesterday at the police station. Marcus admitted that he took the money and tried to make it look like Joe's work, to get him into trouble." He added, "I got the feeling that Joe has always been his parents' favorite. I think Marcus was trying to bring him down in their eyes."

Alex remembered something that Marcus had said to him on Monday, after the softball game: *"They're always saying to me, 'Why can't you be more like Joe?'"*

"I feel sorry for Marcus," Alex said out loud.

"He's a very troubled young man," Mr. Velasquez agreed. "Anyway, he also admitted to ruining your T-shirt, Lenni, and to leaving the two threatening notes. He said he

111

wrote them in code because he figured you all would think it was Joe's doing."

"You mean *three* threatening notes, don't you, Mr. Velasquez?" Casey corrected him. "And the third one wasn't in code."

Mr. Velasquez shook his head. "No, two. He claimed up and down that he had nothing to do with destroying the art projects or leaving that third note."

Jamal and Lenni exchanged a confused glance. "That's kind of weird," Lenni said after a moment. "Who could have done it then?"

"I must say I tend to believe him since he *did* confess to everything else," Mr. Velasquez said. "I'm wondering now if some of the campers might have been responsible for that incident—you know, some sort of camp trick. I'm going to look into the matter myself."

"What about the stuff with the Park Wildlife Center maps?" Hector spoke up. "Did Marcus say anything about that?"

"Marcus took a copy of Joe's map and changed a few things. Then he made copies of his version and mixed them in with Joe's." Mr. Velasquez shook his head. "Again, he wanted to get Joe in trouble. Joe was in charge of the trip to the wildlife center, and Marcus thought that if one or two of the campers should get lost, well . . ."

Jamal glanced around. "Did Joe ever make it here?"

"He decided to stay at home and help his family work

things out," Mr. Velasquez said. "But he'll be with us on Monday for our trip to Camp Wainwright in the Catskills."

"Will he be going by bus with the campers or by bike with us?" Alex asked.

"He'll be on the bus and so will Wendy," Mr. Velasquez replied. "Fiona, Bones, and I will be with you junior counselors on the bike tour, though."

Gaby and Tina came running up to them just then. "I think it's time to get some more footage for our fabulous Robert Moses Beach video," Gaby said breathlessly. "Hey, Mr. Velasquez, maybe we'll interview *you*."

Mr. Velasquez laughed. "Sure, why not? Just don't ask me any tough questions, okay?"

"Tina, let's get the video camera from Wendy," Gaby said, hopping impatiently from foot to foot. "Come on, Mr. Velasquez, let's find you a good spot."

"Be there in a minute," Tina called out. She bent down, reached into her backpack, and pulled something out. It was a photocopy of a hand-drawn comic strip.

"One of the campers did this strip for the *City Sun* Stop Crime In Our Neighborhood contest," Tina explained.

Alex took the comic strip from her and scanned it quickly. It told the story of how he, Lenni, Tina, Jamal, Hector, Casey, and Gaby had caught Marcus red-handed. The final panel read SUPER SEVEN RECOVERS STOLEN MONEY! in bold letters.

"It should really read 'Super Eight,' you know?" Lenni said with a chuckle. "I mean, Ghostwriter deserves lots of credit!" She pulled a pencil out of her backpack, crossed out the SEVEN, and wrote in EIGHT.

The letters on the page began to shimmer and dance just then. When they'd stopped moving around, they said:

Thank you, Team!

Casey stuck one finger in the sand and wrote: "THANK *YOU*, GHOSTWRITER!"

***

Meanwhile, back in the deserted junior counselors' office at Camp Prospect, a piece of paper lay on the floor behind one of the desks, blown there by a breeze from the open window. The paper had been in that spot since the previous day.

Fred, the janitor, shuffled into the room. He closed the window, emptied the trash can into a garbage bag, and began sweeping the floor. When his broom found the piece of paper that lay behind the desk, he swept it out into the open.

"First they mess up my nice, clean floor downstairs, and now they're throwing their trash around wherever they please," Fred grumbled. "Kids!"

He bent down to pick up the piece of paper and threw it into the garbage bag. He didn't bother to look at it. If he had, he would have seen these words:

ONE OF YOU HAS WHAT I WANT
AND I WILL STOP AT NOTHING TO GET IT
BACK!

TO BE CONTINUED . . .

Look for all three *Camp at Your Own Risk* books!

DAYCAMP NIGHTMARE
Camp at Your Own Risk #1

The Ghostwriter Team is psyched about daycamp in New York City—until they start getting threatening messages. Who thinks the team has something valuable? And *what* does the team have?

DISASTER ON WHEELS
Camp at Your Own Risk #2

The older members of the team take off on a three-day bike trip to sleepaway camp in the Catskill Mountains. But someone's still after them and is putting the team in danger by trying to ruin their bike trip.

CREEPY SLEEPAWAY
Camp at Your Own Risk #3

The whole team is together again at sleepaway camp. Will they figure out who's out to get them—and why?